DON'T GO OUT THERE

C000154023

By

Sean Watson

MAPLE
PUBLISHERS

Don't Go Out There!

Author: Sean Watson

Copyright © Sean Watson (2022)

Original Cover Art: Ash Hipperson

Cover Illustration Re-created by: White Magic Studios

The right of Sean Watson to be identified as author of this work has been asserted by the author in accordance with section 77 and 78 of the Copyright, Designs and Patents Act 1988.

First Published in 2022

ISBN 978-1-915492-82-1 (Paperback)
        978-1-915492-83-8 (E-Book)

Book cover design and Book layout by:
        White Magic Studios
        www.whitemagicstudios.co.uk

Published by:
        Maple Publishers
        1 Brunel Way,
        Slough,
        SL1 1FQ, UK
        www.maplepublishers.com

A CIP catalogue record for this title is available from the British Library.

All rights reserved. No part of this book may be reproduced or translated by any form or by any means, electronic or mechanical, including photocopying, recording or by any information storage and retrieval system without written permission from the author.

The views expressed in this work are solely those of the author and do not necessarily reflect the views of the publisher, and the publisher hereby disclaims any responsibility for them.

To my little brother, Adrian.
(1970-1982)

I would like to thank Andrew and Mike, owners of the Tan Hill Inn, and their manager, Maria, for allowing me to use their pub for the backdrop of this story.

This story is loosely based on some factual events:

The Tan Hill Inn and their customers have been snowed in on many occasions, and during a full moon, maybe. The last time they were snowed in was three days in November 2021, which made world news. However, the idea of werewolves being present is completely fictitious... or is it?

I would like to thank friends, who were happy for me to use names, similar to theirs for my characters in this story. Although the characters are not based on anyone alive, dead, or who had been attacked by werewolves.

CONTENTS

Chapter One

It was October, four o'clock on a Friday afternoon, and Tanya Gascoyne, a young woman from Manchester was alone on the Yorkshire Dales. Unusually for autumn, the weather had been hot. The early evening was quite warm, although it had been raining. Tanya was on her way to the Tan Hill Inn, the highest pub in England, secluded on the Yorkshire Dales. She felt the need to park her mobile home and take in the atmosphere, under the moon as dusk drew in. Tanya undressed and picked up a bottle of vodka. She started to dance erotically, offering herself to the moon. She then laid on a large smooth rock, moaning to the moon, she offered herself to her new lunar God. Fuelled by the vodka, she repeatedly submitted herself to the full moon, until she fell asleep.

Tanya, a red head with green eyes, was close to six-feet tall with an Amazonian figure and incredibly attractive with her pale complexion. She was a twenty-five-year-old history student of the classics and early modern Europe. She was also into the occult, especially the beliefs of the Roman empire. As a historian, she had been able to trace her family tree back as far as sixteen-century France. Two ancestors had been executed, Brigitte Garnier was accused of being a witch, and her husband Louis was charged with being a werewolf, which fascinated Tanya. Tanya was studying her PhD on the Roman occult and early modern witchcraft, at the University of East Anglia.

However, Tanya had only been back in England two days before travelling to Yorkshire. With her love of the Roman empire, she had travelled to North Macedonia, once a province of the Eastern Roman Empire. Tanya wanted to find information on the Roman occult for a dissertation she was writing for her PhD. Whilst in North Macedonia, she had survived an attack by some rabid beast, but she had sustained a severe bite on her inner thigh. She, for some reason, had felt that the attack was more sexual than anything else. Ever since the attack, she had felt strangely different, which was reflected in her new lunar desires. Before her journey to Yorkshire, Tanya did consult her doctor about her attack. He had checked her wound, cleaned it, and redressed her thigh, and had given her antibiotics. However, he told her that there was nothing to worry about. She did not believe him.

Tanya was on the Yorkshire Dales, making sense of her new life underneath a full moon, and eager to find a mate who would share her unique desires. She had time on her hands and no need to be anywhere soon, so she could look forward to her new future, however dark it may be. But were these desires for the moon due to her attack, or due to her bloodline? Tanya had not yet experienced the change that would alter her life, maybe because of the clouds in the sky. The weather was changing, and the full moon was hidden by clouds. Although she had not yet metamorphosised into a wolf, she had felt the changes within her body.

Tanya was awoken by the feel of soft rain on her naked body. She laid there for a little while before getting dressed and then headed off to the Tan Hill Inn, which is a lonely pub situated on the top of the Yorkshire Dales, miles from anywhere. The pub sits on the Pennine way, between Richmond and Kirby Stephen, secluded from the rest of the world, especially during harsh winters. A bloodbath could happen here, and no one would know. William Camden, a seventeenth- century travel writer, described the area in his book *Britannia.* Camden wrote, 'Where this Country bordered upon Lancashire, amongst the mountains it is in most places so vast, solitary, unpleasant, and unsightly, so mute and still.' This travel inn has been serving weary travellers on their journey through this secluded place since the seventeenth century. During the autumn and winter months the Yorkshire Dales can be subject to harsh weather. If it were not for the safety of the Tan Hill Inn, many travellers would perish. However, many of the travellers are only there for the alcohol, the food, and the music.

For the last twelve years, the pub has been owned by Deryck and Carol. Deryck, an ex-steel worker, and his wife of thirty years, bought the pub after their youngest of three fled the roost and joined the army. Two years later, their son was killed in Afghanistan which destroyed them. Now, they just subsist for their surviving children, grandchildren, and their extended family, their staff, and customers.

Tanya parked her mobile home in the pub's carpark and headed into the pub. She had picked this pub for the weekend because of the band playing this evening. Ironically, the band were called 'The Wolf Within,' a heavy metal satanic tribute band. Tanya headed straight to the reception, so she could pay for her overnight parking.

"Hello, how much do you charge for parking a mobile home in your car park?"

"£10 an evening, can we take your registration," replied Carol, standing behind the reception.

"Thank you," said Tanya, "should be a good band tonight. Have they played here before?"

"First time... not my kind of music, too loud for me, and too much swearing," replied Carol.

"Oh, ok... you should let your hair down, love," Tanya said as she paid her money. She headed to the bar for a pint and something to eat.

"Cheek, how rude," answered Carol to herself.

Tanya walked to the bar, managed by Carol's husband, Deryck.

"Hello, my dear, how can I help?"

"Can I have a pint of your strongest ale, please," replied Tanya, "and can I order a sirloin steak, please."

"Sure, how would you like your steak cooked?"

"Blue, thanks... would it be possible to eat in one of your domes, please?"

"In this weather?" asked Deryck.

"Yes, please."

"Yes, sure, here's a key to number two. Sam will bring your food out to you."

"Thank you, can I have another pint as well, please," replied Tanya.

Deryck poured her another pint, and she then headed outside to the dome.

She sat in the dome, enjoying her pint and the night sky, with the pitta-patter of rain on the glass. There was no visible moon, but she felt the urge to change. Suddenly, the door opened, there stood a young woman holding a plate of food.

"Hello sexy, how can I help?" asked Tanya.

"What? Um, yes, um, here's your steak, madam," replied Sam, who was now feeling quite nervous about the customer she had served, "can I get you anything else?"

"Another pint of your strongest ale please. What time does the band start?"

"Eight o'clock in the function room, I'll get your drink. Enjoy your meal, madam."

"Why not join me," said Tanya as she pattered the chair next to her.

"Sorry, I must get back to work."

Sam returned to the pub, she asked Deryck for a pint of what Tanya was drinking.

"Deryck, could you take the pint to her, please?" asked Sam, "she makes me nervous... I think she's going to pounce on me?"

"Ok, keep an eye on the bar while I've gone... wish me luck, Sam," Deryck laughed, "she might pounce on me?"

"Ha-ha. Deryck, you'll see what I mean when you get out there."

"Just a lonely young woman looking for some company," replied Deryck.

"Well, she's not going to be looking for your company... you old fart," said Carol as she walked through from the reception.

She and Sam laughed as Deryck stuck his fingers up at them both, smiling, "how rude!" He then left the bar to take the pint to Tanya. Once outside, Deryck used his tray to cover the pint from the rain as he walked to the dome.

"Hello again, young lady... here is your pint... how is your food."

"Oh, the sexy young waitress has been changed for an older man, how nice," smiled Tanya, "the food is lovely, thank you."

"Sam had other tables to serve," Deryck hesitated, "someone will check on you in a little while. Should they bring you a dessert menu?"

"No thanks, I'm not a sweet kind of girl," smiled Tanya.

"Ok, enjoy your evening," replied Deryck as he collected the empty glasses, returned to the bar, and re-joined Sam and Carol.

"I see what you mean... there is something weird about her, Sam," said Deryck, "she's not having anything else, so wait till she comes in before you go and collect the plates... it's still raining out there."

An hour passed when Sam returned to the dome to retrieve Tanya's dirty plate. Tanya had left to go and watch the music, which had started playing. About forty guests had gathered near the stage for the music. Tanya had noticed one man who tapped to the music whilst he sat on his own. She walked to the bar in the function room, which was tended by Simon and Clare.

"Hiya, can I have a pint of 'Granny Wouldn't Like It' please? Unusual name... nice pint, though."

"Yes, the owners have just come back from two weeks' holiday in Norfolk," replied Simon, "normal people bring back sticks of rock... they brought back two barrels of this. It's from the Wolf Brewery near Norwich."

"Interesting," said Tanya.

Tanya walked over to the man sitting on his own. He looked scruffy with a beard, wearing denim, he was dressed for the band, but he did not look like the type of man that Tanya would like. She wore designer clothes and looked incredibly attractive. Tanya had joined the young because he was on his own.

"Do you mind if I join you, Sir... I'm Tanya," she said as she offered her hand.

"I'm Jack. I'm pleased to meet you," smiled the young man as he shook her hand, "you not enjoying the music?"

"Yes, love them, but I don't like crowds," replied Tanya, "don't you like them?"

"I do like them... I work for them, the band," answered Jack, "I'm their roadie... I'm not keen on crowds either."

"Interesting... are they a busy band?"

"Yes, they tour Europe and do some of the festivals," replied Jack, "I tend to help them on smaller gigs like this. I've been around Europe with them as well... it pays the bills."

"You finished for the night, or have you got to pack up later?" Tanya asked.

"No, we leave everything in here till the morning... securer than in the van."

The pair chatted for another hour or so before leaving. Tanya took Jack back to her mobile home and opened a bottle of whiskey.

"Would you like one of these?" asked Tanya as she stood with her back to Jack, slipping something into his drink.

"What? Oh, yes please," replied Jack as he was admiring the ornaments on Tanya's wall, "these Samurai swords are nice."

"Yes. They are my brother's."

After a couple of glasses, Jack felt lightheaded and collapsed on the sofa.

The next morning, Jack woke up late and felt terrible. He did not feel hungover, but as if he had been drugged. Jack rushed out of the vehicle to find a stone wall to vomit over. The sight that he was met with made him sick again. On the

11

other side of the wall was a dead sheep, which looked like it had been attacked and eaten by a large dog. Jack rushed back into the motor home to find Tanya, but she was not there. There was no evidence that she had slept in the vehicle, and the bedding was still folded. On the table, there was a note with a set of keys sitting on it. The note was also smeared with blood.

"See you soon," Jack read to himself, "what the fuck, maybe she is in the pub."

"What the fuck are you doing in here," said Oz, one of the band members, who stood at the door, "thanks for the help this morning."

"Sorry Oz, I think I was drugged last night," replied Jack, "have you seen Tanya?"

"Who?"

"The woman I was with last night… who owns this motor home."

"No idea what you are on about Jack," said Oz as he headed back to the band's van, "Oh, you're not getting paid for this morning."

"Ok," replied Jack as he stuck his fingers up behind Oz's back.

Jack then freshened up and got dressed before heading to the pub for breakfast. Some of the guests were already in the bar, eating, but Tanya was nowhere to be seen. Jack sat down, and Sam came over to take his order.

"What would you like, sir?"

"I'll just have a pot of tea and an orange juice, please… not feeling too great this morning," answered Jack, "have you seen Tanya, the woman whose motor home is near the wall?"

"Tanya, the weird woman… I haven't seen her since last night," replied Sam.

"I wonder where she has gone?... Oh, there's a dead sheep on the other side of that wall near her motor home," said Jack, "looks as though a dog has killed it."

"Not another one? We found two in the backfield behind the pub. We have been in touch with the farmer."

"Oh, ok," replied Jack, "but where has she gone?"

"Have you checked her motor home?"

"Um, yeah... maybe I'll check again."

Sam returned to the bar to get Jack's order. When she revisited Jack's table with his drinks, he had left. Jack had gone back to Tanya's van to see if she had returned, but Tanya was nowhere to be seen. As he stood near the letter that she had written, he picked up the keys.

"These must be the keys to this van?" he said to himself as he juggled with them, wondering where she could be. Jack then noticed what the keys had been hiding on Tanya's letter, 'PTO.'

He turned the piece of paper over, and it read, 'Jack, keep my van. I will find you. This is my number. Look after my van, I will see you soon. Everything is ok. I will explain next time I see you. Do not tell anyone about this! Tanya.'

"How strange. What on earth is she on about?"

There was a bit of blood smeared on this side of the paper too, just under where she had written her number. Jack quickly put the piece of paper in his pocket, just in case someone was watching. He sat in the driver's seat with the keys in his hand, pondering on what to do next. He got up and rushed over to the bands van to grab his stuff, luckily the band were still at breakfast. Jack noticed an envelope of money, with the band's name on it.

"This must be my wages?" he said to himself as he checked if anyone was watching.

13

He spotted James, one of the chefs, standing near the pub, smoking. He waved to him with the envelope in his hand, and James waved back. Jack headed back to the mobile home, threw his bag and the envelope onto the sofa, and started the engine. He retrieved the note from his pocket, dialled the number, but there was no answer. A few minutes later he received a message from the same number, 'I now have your number. I'll be in touch soon. Remember, do not tell anyone.' This confused Jack, "what the hell is going on?"

Without telling anyone, he left the car park in Tanya's vehicle and headed home, back to Leeds, or maybe somewhere else, maybe.

When the band got back to their van, they noticed that the envelope had gone, as well as Tanya's mobile home.

"That prick has nicked our money," said Oz.

The band, after a bit of swearing, went back into the pub. They walked up to the reception where Carol was sitting, and they told her what had happened.

"Do you have the registration of that womens van, please? They have nicked our money."

"Would you like me to call the police?"

"No thanks, we'll get him."

Carol read out the registration number to them.

Oz shook his head, "No, not our reg. The one for that woman, Tanya."

"That was the one she wrote down."

"Really. She gave you our reg, and you didn't check it. Great, now what we going to do?"

Chapter Two

A month later, close to the next full moon, Karl and Brad had flown to Europe. Karl and Brad were twins, and their family were wealthy cattle farmers from Lubbock, Texas. Karl, the older twin, was bigger than Brad, but both were athletic and about six foot tall. Karl played American football at college, so was more muscular than Brad, who preferred baseball. They were identical twins with brown hair and brown eyes. Brad was hairy all over, but Karl was not as hairy as his brother. The Texan twins had decided to backpack around Europe during their gap year. After their sabbatical, the pair intend to do PhD's in their selected subjects. Brad's was sports science, and Karl's was geography. As Americans with an English, French, and Polish heritage, they wanted to learn more about the culture and history of Europe at first hand.

First stop, London, England, they had just landed at Heathrow. Exhausted from their journey, the pair had collected their luggage and passed through customs. Although tired, the brothers were excited about their travels and the adventures they will have along the way. They were laughing and joking as they headed out of the airport. They hoped to travel more of England than just London during their two-weeks break in the UK, including a stay at the Tan Hill Inn, on the Yorkshire Dales. Laden with just their backpacks, they waited outside the airport for a taxi to take them to Kings Cross station.

"Karl, come on, there's a taxi over there," Brad shouted as he ran across the road, ignoring the direction of the traffic in this foreign country.

"Brad... wait!" shouted a shocked Karl as Brad was struck by another taxi that he had not seen. As the taxi hit Brad, he was flung into a parked car. Whilst braking, the cab still travelled past the parked car. Brad's leg was trapped between the two vehicles, which forced him to the ground, headfirst. His head, neck and then back took the full force of the concrete, which knocked him unconscious.

"Brad, Brad!" Karl ran to his brothers' side as a crowd gathered, "Please, someone call for an ambulance!"

"I'm sorry, he just ran out in front of me!" explained a very apologetic taxi driver, who was on his phone to the emergency services.

Within minutes the paramedics arrived at the scene.

Two paramedics ran over to Brad, "let us through, please, give us some space... can anyone tell us what happened?"

Everyone who had gathered, started shouting what they had seen, which made no sense to the paramedics.

"Stop, one at a time!" explained one of the paramedics. "You. You and he must be twins?" the other paramedic asked Karl as he checked Brad's breathing and pulse, "what happened?"

"Yes, we were looking for a cab... when he just ran out in front of this guy."

"He just ran out in front of me... I had no time to brake... I was only doing about twenty miles an hour," replied the taxi driver.

Both paramedics looked at each other as they looked after their patient, Brad.

"It is only ten miles an hour along this road, sir," answered a police officer, who had been nearby controlling the crowd, "we'll have to have a chat?" as the police officer led the taxi driver to his car.

The paramedics continued with Brad, bracing his neck and back. Brad and Karl were soon in the ambulance heading to Hillingdon Hospital, which was the nearest to Heathrow airport.

Brad woke up in hospital, with Karl sitting next to his bed. Brad was in some pain, but the medication was helping. However, he was feeling a bit groggy.

"What the fuck... where am I... what happened?"

"You're in hospital, buddy, ... you got hit by a cab as we came out of the airport," Karl explained, then chuckling, "I know I said catch that cab, but not like that!"

"That fucking Limey was driving on the wrong side of the road," whispered Brad, careful about the nurse not to hear.

She replied, smiling, "we all drive on that side of the road over here. How are you feeling? I need you to take these tablets after your lunch. Choose from the menu, and I'll get it ordered for you."

Karl asked, "Can I have anything?"

The nurse said sarcastically, "yes, anything your brother leaves you."

"You're all heart... I'm starving," replied Karl, "what's your name?"

"Why? You going to complain to my superiors?" asked the nurse.

"No, just interested!"

"Lucy, it's on my badge," she replied, "there is a café on the ground floor for visitors... that's the best I can do, I'm afraid!"

"Alright, you two, chatting each other up," shouted Brad, "I'm still here."

"I don't think so," Lucy replied as she picked up Brad's menu, "ahh, the fish and chips, excellent choice."

"Mmm, British gourmet food," laughed Karl.

"Better than those hamburgers with no ham, you lot are famous for." As she left the room, Lucy said, "Doctor Asker will be in to check on you soon... I'll check in with you after lunch."

Now, Lucy was of a similar age to the brothers. She was five feet tall, slim, with blonde hair and blue eyes.

The two brothers looked at each other as the nurse left the room.

"She's nice!" said Brad, still groggy from the morphine.

"Well, she's a beautiful English rose. Pity she's not interested... I think I have upset her there," surmised Karl, "How are you feeling bro, you in pain?... I've rung mum and dad!"

"I think you did upset her, bud... I'm ok, a bit sore, but feeling good on this medication," replied Brad. "How were mum and dad?

"Worried about you, I've assured them that you will live," said Karl

"Good day, gentlemen. Your brother is correct, you will live," explained Brad's Doctor, Doctor Asker as he walked into the room.

"When can I leave, Doc?"

Going through his patient's notes, the Doctor replied, "I'm afraid you will be with us for at least one weeks... You have a broken ankle, as well as a fractured wrist. We are more concerned about the severe bruising and swelling on your back and your neck, which we need to monitor," replied Doctor Asker. "I'll be in to see you later this afternoon."

Shaking the brother's hands, Doctor Asker then left the room.

"Fuck sake, we're supposed to be getting that train up to Yorkshire. The room is booked at the Tan Hill Inn, and I'm stuck in hospital in this godforsaken country for the week." Brad shouted, frustrated with his current situation rather than England.

"Calm down, Brad. We can go up there later when you are back on your feet!"

"No, you wanted to be there for the full moon... you'll miss that Ska band you were looking forward to seeing at the Pub," said Brad. "You go up there on your own. I can join you when I'm on my feet. I'm in the best place, with Lucy looking after me?" Brad winked at his brother.

"Are you sure? Never did fancy staying in London."

"Cheers, you can't wait to go now!" laughed Brad.

"You know what I'm like in big cities... will you be ok?"

"What time was the train for Richmond for?" asked Brad.

"Four O'clock from King Cross to Darlington. We also have that hotel booked for the night in Darlington. Then tomorrow morning, a bus to Richmond. We were going to hike to the pub, weren't we? I'm looking forward to that," Karl replied.

"You better head off then."

"Are you sure you don't mind?"

19

"No, go... enjoy yourself. I'll catch up with you when I'm out of here."

"Are you sure?... I can wait for you, Brad."

"Yes, go, fuck off."

"Ok, I'll see you soon... love you, bro!" Karl shouted as he picked up his backpack and ran out of the room, nearly knocking Lucy off her feet, "Brad, I'll call you when I'm on the train."

"Blimey, slow down. You'll end up in a bed next to your brother!" snapped Lucy, "and be quiet... This is a hospital, not a football pitch."

"Sorry Lucy... Look after him for me, please!" replied Karl, as he walked along the corridor.

"Where is he off to, Brad?"

"Yorkshire... we had train and room booked, no point losing both tickets... He was looking forward to this part of the trip."

"Why Yorkshire?" asked Lucy, "where else were you travelling to?"

"Why, you want to join us?" Brad smiled. "We were going to stay at the Tan Hill Inn, near Richmond, Yorkshire, before heading up to Scotland, then over to Dublin, before heading into Europe via Paris, and finishing in East Europe."

"Wow sounds like fun... we used to go to Yorkshire a lot as kids. We have camped at that pub, many times," Lucy answered, "how are you feeling?"

"I'm ok, feeling tired!"

"Get some sleep. I will be in later with the Doctor."

"Thanks, Lucy."

Chapter Three

Karl's taxi had dropped him off at Kings Cross station within an hour of leaving the hospital. He headed towards the nearest ticket booth.

"Hiya, I wonder if you can help me… I've got two tickets for Richmond, Yorkshire. The information is on my phone. Can I reserve my brother's ticket for a later date?"

"I think we can do that for you, sir. Can I have your phone for the details, please?" the ticket officer replied whilst taking Karl's phone. He tapped in the information he needed to prolong Brad's ticket use.

"All sorted, sir, the ticket is safe for a month. However, your brother will need to confirm his travel date with us. He will need to do this within the next three days."

"Thanks for that… I'll let my brother know when I call him later."

"That's ok. Can I help you with anything else, sir?"

"No thanks, you have been more than helpful. Again, thank you," replied Karl.

"You are more than welcome, have a pleasant journey, sir."

Karl had a couple hours to kill before his train arrived, and he still had not eaten, so he headed to the station's bar for lunch and a pint or two.

"Hiya, can I please have a pint of your best English ale and a menu?"

"Here you go, try this," said the bartender as he gave Karl a pint of an amber ale.

"Wow, that's nice. I can get used to your ales," replied Karl as he looked at the menu, "Oh, and can I order your gourmet burger too, please, Steve?" pointing to the bartender's badge.

"Of course, that will be £23.50, please."

"Thanks. Is it ok to sit at the bar?"

"Yes, no problem, sir," replied Steve.

Karl searched his pockets for his phone, "Shit, where's that gone?"

"Where's what gone, sir?" Steve replied.

"I've lost my phone."

At that point, he felt a tap on his shoulder. He turned to see the chap from the ticket office, waving Karl's phone. "Did you forget something, sir?"

"Blimey, as you English would say. Thank you for that... I would forget my head if it were loose."

The ticket officer placed the phone on the bar next to Karl and returned to his ticket booth. Karl gave his brother a call, and Lucy answered.

"Hello, is that Karl? This is Lucy, your brother's nurse. He's asleep at the moment."

"Is he ok?"

"He's ok, tired. I'll let him know you rang when he wakes."

"Thanks... Oh, Lucy!"

"Yes, still here."

"Can you tell him that his train ticket is open for a month?" replied Karl, "I'll explain to him later when I talk to him."

"I'll let him know, Karl."

"Thanks, Lucy, look after him for me, please?"

Karl then finished the call and continued to eat his burger and finished his pint.

"Can I have another pint, please, Steve?"

"Here you go, sir, try this one!" replied Steve.

"Mmm, that's nice, so is that burger. You English know how to cook a mean burger!"

Karl spent the next hour chatting with Steve. They talked about his travels around Europe. They also talked about where they would love to visit. Steve had told Karl that he intended to travel the US when he had saved enough money. The two also realised that they would be skiing in the Alps simultaneously during the following spring. On leaving, Karl gave his number to Steve before heading off to his platform for the train.

"Thanks, Steve. Here's my number," said Karl. "Let me know when you are in France. You'll meet my brother, Brad."

"Cheers, Karl, enjoy the rest of your trip. See you in France," replied Steve.

Due to his time spent at the bar, Karl did not have long to wait for his train. Now settled in his seat, he felt tired because of the day he and his brother had had since getting off the plane that morning. It was not long before he fell asleep. Half an hour into his journey, the ticket conductor suddenly awakened him, "can I see your ticket, please sir"

Feeling fatigued, he produced his phone with the online ticket to the ticket conductor.

"Thank you, sir," as the ticket collector walked to the next passenger.

It was not long before Karl had fallen asleep again. He was awoken by the Tannoy announcement from the driver.

"Ladies and gentlemen, our next stop will be Darlington, which should be in the next fifteen minutes. Have all your items with you before leaving the train. Thank you."

Karl stretched his arms and rubbed the sleep from his eyes. He then spotted the young child opposite copying him, "cheeky!" Karl smiled.

"You slept well there, mate," replied the little boy's father.

"That was the first chance of sleep since landing at Heathrow this morning," said Karl, "he's a cheeky one?"

"He is... I don't know where he gets it from?" said the dad, "I'm Peter."

"How are you? I'm Karl," as he shook Peter's hand.

"Oh, you're American?"

"Yes I am. You and your son going on vacation?"

"No, not really. I'm dropping him off at my parents in Kendal," replied Peter as he looked at his son, "we are going to Darlington first to take him to see his mother's grave."

"Oh, man. I'm sorry to hear that," said Karl, "are you then off to work after you have dropped your son off?"

"No, I'm heading to Richmond to try and find my sister, Tanya," replied Peter.

"Oh. I'm heading to Richmond too, before going to a pub on the Yorkshire Dales."

"The Tan Hill Inn?" asked Peter.

"Yes... you've been before?" replied Karl.

"Yes, a few times, with my sister. We grew up in Kirby Stephen, before my parents moved to Kendal, in Cumbria."

"Oh, cool... so what happened to your sister?"

"We don't know... she normally keeps in touch with our parents, but they haven't heard from her ever since she

24

returned from North Macedonia. I have received one message from her, but it was vague. She just said she was close to our favourite place ever. Which is that pub."

"Oh, I hope you have some luck finding her," said Karl, "tell you what, why don't we swap numbers? If I hear anything, I can let you know."

"Cheers, thanks for that," replied Peter as they swapped phone numbers, "Oh, if you are lucky to meet her, can you tell her that I would like my Samurai swords back."

"Oh, ok. No worries. I hope I can help," said Karl. "It must be hard for you, being a single parent. Must be hard on him to, not having his mother around?

"It has been hard on us both. He's ok, though. He's a good lad, really. Come on, Sean. Say goodbye to the man."

"Goodbye, mister!" came the little voice.

"See you, mate. See you Peter... good luck," replied Karl as he put his backpack on and headed for the exit, as the train pulled into the station.

Karl stepped onto the platform and pulled out his phone to look at the time, "it's seven O'clock... oh, a text message from Brad. What's he got to say?"

"Are you in Darlington yet? Call when you are there... looks like I might be stuck in London for longer than we hoped... Lucy says hiya, wink," as Karl read his brother's message.

"Better call him!" Karl said to himself as he called Brad. "Hiya Brad, how are you doing, buddy? Can you hear me?"

"Yes, I can hear you, bro. I'm ok. The Doctor is still concerned about the swelling in my back and neck, though.... I'm a bit spaced out on these drugs at the moment." Brad put his phone on loudspeaker.

"Is that nurse looking after you?"

"Yes, she is, and she's single."

"Shut up! I won't give you any more drugs."

"Lucy, get my brother back on his feet, please," Karl shouted. "Look, Brad, I'm going to go. I'm just across the road from the hotel in Darlington. I'm tired, starving, and I need a drink. I'll speak to you tomorrow."

"Ok, Karl, have a couple for me. I'll chat with you tomorrow."

As Karl walked into the hotel, he viewed the bar on his right. With the idea of beer making his mouth water, he walked straight to reception. "Hiya, I've got a room booked under the name of Brad and Karl Kaminsky."

"You're American?"

"I am!"

"There's only one of you, sir?"

"No, there are millions of us," came the sarcastic response.

"No, I meant only one for your room?" said the receptionist.

"There is... you English are very observant!"

"Sorry, sir."

"No, that's ok...my brother's still in London. He's stuck in a hospital. He was hit by a taxi at Heathrow," smiled Karl.

"Ouch, not the best way to catch a cab. Here's your keys, sir."

"Thanks, would it be possible for someone to take my bag to my room, please?... I need a drink... are you still serving food?"

"Yes, and yes, sir," replied the receptionist.

"Thanks," said Karl as he walked towards the bar.

"Can I have a pint of your best ale and a sirloin steak, please," asked Karl to the bartender.

"How would you like your steak cooked?" replied the bartender.

"Well done, please... oh, and all the trimmings, please."

"Ok, sir, here's your pint. Take a seat, and I'll bring your food over to you, sir."

"Thanks... I'm in room two. Can you put it on my room bill, please?"

"Ok, sir. I'll be over with your food as soon as it is ready, sir," the bartender replied.

"Thanks."

Half an hour after Karl had sat down, the bartender brought over his food.

"Here you go, sir."

"Oh, thanks. That looks great," said Karl.

"Anything else, sir?"

"Another pint, please."

The bartender went back to the bar and returned with a pint for Karl.

"Here you go, sir. Enjoy!"

"Thank you!"

Karl finished his dinner and then went to his room, where his bag sat waiting for him. As soon as his head hit the pillow, he was out like a light.

Following morning, Karl awoke, still feeling jet lagged. He phoned reception to arrange another night in his room and asked not to be disturbed. As he finished on the phone to reception, his mobile rang. It was Brad.

"Hiya Brad, how are you doing?"

"I'm ok. I have had a good night's sleep. I've just had a British fry up," said Brad. "I'm still in pain, but Lucy's drugs are working. How's you?"

"I'm still knackered, still in bed. I'm staying here today. I'll head over to Richmond and the Tan Hill Inn, tomorrow... I'm going to sleep all day. You know what I'm like... how are you?" repeated Karl as he nearly fell asleep.

"Yes, I'm ok. I spoke to mum and dad last night, after I spoke to you. They send their love."

"Oh, good... Are they ok?"

"They are ok. I'll let you get back to sleep, you keep dropping off. Speak to you tomorrow, bye."

"Speak later. I'll call you tomorrow."

It is not long before Karl fell back to sleep.

The following morning, Karl awoke feeling refreshed but very hungry. He made himself a coffee, and whilst munching on one of the complimentary biscuits, he called reception. "Hello, it's Mr Kaminsky from room two... What time is breakfast served until, please?"

"Morning, Mr Kaminsky. How was your sleep? Breakfast finishes at 9:30. It is now 8:30, you have plenty of time, sir," replied the receptionist.

"Great. I slept very well, thank you... I'll be down in about half an hour."

Karl had his shower and headed down to reception to drop off his key. He then walked through to where he had eaten two nights ago.

"Can I help you, sir?"

"Fresh coffee, please. My brother recommended a British fry-up. Mind you, he had his in hospital."

The waiter smiled, "I'll bring you over your full English breakfast. All the trimmings?"

"Yes, please," replied Karl.

Ten minutes later, the waiter brings over Karl's breakfast. "Here we go, sir."

"Thank you."

"Anything else, sir?"

"No thanks," replied Karl as he looked up from the local paper he had picked up, "Just been reading about this girl who went missing near Richmond the other month. What happened?"

"No one knows. A body has not been found yet… seems she was a bit of a loner, with no family. It seems like the police have lost interest."

"That's terrible!" said Karl

"She went missing out on the dales, near the Tan Hill Inn, during the full moon." replied the waiter, "I think she is still alive, personally… enjoy your breakfast." The waiter then headed over to some other guests.

"I wonder if that was that peter's sister?" Karl said to himself as he read the article. "She was last seen with one man, who also disappeared. This man stole some money as well. Oh, she left the wrong details at the pub as well."

Karl left the hotel to make his way to Richmond. He had decided to hail a cab. Looking at his watch.

"it's now 11:40. How the hell do you get a taxi around here," he said to himself as he looked for one.

"You won't get a taxi like that around here, pet," said an elderly lady in her broad Yorkshire accent.

"Thanks… where can I get a taxi from, please."

"You are American, pet? My aunty was in the company of many of you during the war... she used to get a lot of money off them," the old lady said, fondly remembering her aunty. "Just across the road, you can get a taxi there, love."

"Thank you," replied Karl as he ran across the road, looking confused as he heard the old lady say, "You should be careful when you get to the Yorkshire Dales, pet...Don't go out there... He won't live!"

"How did she know where I'm going?" he thought to himself as he entered the taxi rank. Karl walked to the window of the office where a woman sat, tapping her pen to the music, playing on the radio.

"Morning, sir, can I help you?" she asked as she looked up at Karl.

"Hiya, can I have a cab to Richmond, please?"

"Yes, pet. Take a seat, it'll be about half an hour." Then the lady spoke into the radio, "Jim, where are you? Can you do a drop to Richmond asap, please, from the office?" looking up at Karl, "An American."

"Oh, remember the Alamo!" said the voice.

"And threw out the Mexican," she replied, smiling at Karl.

"Ha-ha, the joke from the film, American Werewolf in London?" enquired Karl, "love that film."

The taxi operator gave him a thumbs up. Karl returned the thumbs up, then sat down.

"How long, Jim?"

"On my way, about ten minutes."

"Ok, cool."

"Taxi for Richmond?" came a voice from the entrance.

"That was quick!"

"I've been standing here all that time," Jim smiled sarcastically, "Come on then... time is money," Jim said to Karl. Jim then turned and walked back to his car. Karl followed Jim and climbed into the passenger's seat.

"Where to in Richmond?" Jim asked.

"Nearest café that you can recommend, please?" replied Karl, "do you mind if I join you in the front, Jim?"

"No, fill your boots... I know just the place," Jim said as he drove off.

During their journey, they chatted about Karl's travels and his brother.

"How long is your brother stuck in hospital?" asked Jim.

"He might be there for one or two weeks," Karl replied.

"Blimey, how long are you in England?"

"I'll stay in Yorkshire until he can join me," Karl explained, "we were planning to spend time at the highest pub in Britain."

"Nice pub, great food. You will have an exciting time there, with Carol and Deryck," said Jim. "Bloody cold this time of year though... you don't want to find yourself lost on them Yorkshire dales at night!" Jim warned, "Don't go out there. Could be deadly."

"I'm sure everything will be fine. I can't wait to get there."

"Here you go, best breakfast in North Yorkshire... not that I've tried all of them," Jim laughed as he stopped outside a café, called Granny's Kitchen.

As Karl headed to the door of the café, Jim warned him, "Hey, Karl, I'd give it a couple of days before you head up to the Tan Hill Inn... it's a full moon the next couple of nights, cold up there this time of year," then he drove off.

A confused Karl said, "oh, ok!" he then said to himself, "what the fuck was that all about… weird, first the old lady, and now Jim. Oh well," Karl shrugged it off as he went into the café.

He walked up to the girl behind the counter. He looked at her name badge, and asked, "morning Claire, I have a gap to fill in my belly after my fry-up earlier. What do you recommend?"

"How about one of our cream teas, sir?"

"Ok, no idea what one of those is. Sounds nice, and I'm tempted, but I'll just have some toast and a latte, please."

"Excellent. Take a seat, and I'll bring it over, sir."

"Thank you, nice to see someone so beautiful on such a dreary morning," Karl said.

Claire smiled embarrassingly, "Thank you, sir."

"That's ok… call me Karl. You lived here all your life?"

"No, I moved here from Plymouth with my ex."

"Where is Plymouth?" Karl asked, smiling.

"Down in Devon."

"Nice part of the country?" asked Karl, "Maybe I should visit, sometime?"

"You should, it's a lovely part of the country," Claire smiled back as Karl went to find somewhere to sit.

Karl found a comfy looking sofa hidden in the corner and sat down. He pulled out his road map of the UK and the one of Europe from his backpack.

"Oh shit, I've got Brad's as well. Right, how far am I away from the pub now. I might need a bus," as he flicked through the index and then for the page he needed.

"Oh, thought I was closer than this… should have got Jim to drop me off there."

Claire brought over Karl's latte and toast and placed them on the table in front of him. Karl asked her, "is there a bus that passes the Tan Hill Inn?"

"No, there's a bus that goes to Kirby Stephen, which can drop you off nearby, but I wouldn't make that trip this time of year. It'll be foggy on the dales this afternoon, plus it's a full moon tonight."

"What is it with you people and the full moon?" Karl asked.

"Just not a delightful place to get lost... out there, on them dales... Don't go out there! I wouldn't," Claire replied.

Ignoring Claire's concerns, he asked her where and what time he can catch a bus going in that direction?

"The next one will be about 2:30, there, opposite the café... there's one every two hours this time of year, and the last one is at 6:30."

"Thanks!"

Karl was suddenly tapped on the shoulder, "sorry, didn't realise you were here, you must have fallen asleep!" came a male voice.

"Where's Claire... what's the time?" Karl said as he wiped his eyes.

The waiter replied, "she finished at two... it's now about 4:15."

"Shit, I've missed the fucking bus."

"No, it will be here at 4:30... across the road there."

"Cheers, I meant the 2:30 bus!"

"Oh, yes, you have missed that one."

Karl gave the waiter cash for his bill, grabbed his bag, and ran for the door, "keep the change."

Karl made his way to the other side of the road and waited for about ten minutes at the bus stop. Karl thought to himself that he should leave it till tomorrow.

"I might meet Claire in one of her local pubs, tonight, if I stay?" he said as the bus pulled up. He hesitated, and then he got on the bus. He was the only passenger on there.

"Not many customers today, sir?"

"No, sir," the driver replied, "no one in their right mind would want to travel through the dales this time of day or year."

Karl hesitated again, thinking of the possibility of meeting Claire if he stayed another night.

"Where are you going, sir?"

Karl looked at the driver with a determination, "how close can you get me to the Tan Hill Inn?"

"You must be mad, don't go out there tonight."

"No, come on, let's do this... think me as your wingman, get me as close as you can," shouted an enthusiastic Karl.

"I can drop you off near a place called Keld, then it's probably about a five-mile walk north to the Tan Hill for you. A road will take you to a T junction, then you'll need to turn right... you can't miss the pub," replied a not so enthusiastic driver, "keep on the road though... it will be foggy later, and you could easily get lost out there!"

Karl sat down on the lonely bus, and the driver pulled away. The driver then suddenly stopped to let someone else on. A figure in an oversized warm coat got on and said to the driver, "I'm going wherever he's going!" as the figure turned to Karl.

"Claire, what are you doing here?"

"I saw you on the bus and thought I'd join you... is that ok?" Claire said as she walked over and sat next to him.

"Thought you said you wouldn't take this trip this time of year... but hay, yeah, cool, great,... great to see you... glad I fell asleep in your café now," Karl explained to her as she laughed and then smiled at him.

"Tell me more about why you are in Yorkshire?"

"Ok, I followed a dick of a bloke up here who I met at home in Plymouth while he was working there... fucking wanker was married."

"Oops, and you stayed near him?"

"No, he and his poor wife are in Leeds... He had moved me into a flat in Bradford... I moved to Richmond straight away and fell in love with the place, been here since June last year."

Karl smiled, "Well, I'm glad he was a dick... I would never have met you if he had been a nice bloke."

Karl and Claire sat there enjoying each other's company when Karl's phone suddenly rang.

"My brother... nearly forgot about him. Let me just take this," he said to Claire. "Hiya Brad, how are you doing, bro? How's Lucy?"

"I'm ok, still in pain. Lucy is looking after me... How are you doing. What's the highest pub in Britain like?" came the voice from Karl's phone.

"Not there yet, now on a bus heading there."

"A bus dropping you off at a pub, cool."

"No, got about a five-mile hike across the dales, to the pub."

"Fuck, and you're on your way there tonight?... are you mad?" replied Brad.

"I'll be ok, got a local joining me, her name is Claire. Anyway, what's the doc said, when are you getting up here?" asked Karl, eager to be with his twin again, "bring Lucy with you."

"Still not sure how long, still waiting for the swelling to go down. I'll let you know," replied Brad, "Lucy's just walked in with my medication. Let me know when you get to the pub. Stay safe... and tell me more about Claire. Speak later." Then Brad hung up his phone.

"See you soon, bro... oh, he's gone."

Chapter Four

An hour into the journey, there was a shout from the driver, "here's your stop!"

Both Karl and Claire got up and headed to the front of the bus.

"You guys be careful. Looks like fog is setting in... should keep you safe from the full moon!"

"WHAT, I think you people around here watch too many Lon Chaney films!" replied Karl, "thanks for dropping us off here."

"There is a campsite here, where you could stay at."

"I have a room already booked at the Tan Hill."

"Ok, just follow Stonesdale lane, north," the driver replied, "about five miles, you'll come to the Pennine Way. Turn right, and the pub is there on your left... You can't miss it."

As the pair stepped off the bus, the driver shouted, "make sure you keep on the road."

Karl and Claire waved as the bus pulled away. They watched as it disappeared into the fog. Karl and Claire started walking up Stonesdale lane, Karl pulled his torch from his backpack.

"Well, this is nice," whispered Karl, "what made you get on the bus? I'm glad you did though."

"I'll be honest with you, Karl, I fancied you the first time I saw you in the café, and when I saw you on the bus, I thought fuck it, I've got some time off work, let's get away from here," laughed Claire, "didn't pack anything though."

Now, Claire was an attractive woman who was quite tall with an athletic body. Underneath her warm coat, she was wearing a short black dress, and she was wearing high heels. Before getting on the bus, she was going to meet with friends in the Golden Lion, in Richmond.

"Wow, you look stunning as well. I fancy you too."

Claire pulled Karl towards her and kissed him full on the lips, a full French kiss which lasted for a good couple of minutes. They started to walk north hand in hand in what they hoped, was the direction of the pub. The couple walked for another half an hour before stopping again for a kiss, this time more intensely.

"I'm afraid we only have one room at the inn, but it has two single beds."

"That's ok. We can push the beds together," replied Claire as she pulled Karl to her and unzipped his trousers. They stepped off the road and walked to a large tree. The couple settled under the tree and explored each other's bodies in the fog. As they undressed, Karl pulled a sleeping bag from his backpack, "this will keep us warm. It's also a double, handy, hey?" he laughed.

"You came prepared!" laughed Claire as she removed her large coat, "you were planning this situation?"

"Quickly, get in here before you freeze," Karl smiled and then winked at Claire as they climbed into the sleeping bag.

Karl suddenly woke up and looked at his watch, "Shit, we better get moving. It's 10:30... we must have fallen asleep." Luckily, Karl had deliberately laid his backpack pointing north, hopefully in the direction of the pub. They got up, dressed, and sorted themselves out. kissed and started walking north. Karl offered Claire a pair of salopettes, socks, and some trainers to keep her warm, and help her walk on the dales.

"I'm ok. You have warmed me up nicely, and I don't like anything else on my feet. I'll put those on though," as she took the salopettes.

"Ok, your choice. Come on, Claire, this way!" said Karl.

"Are you sure?"

"Positive... think so... yes, I'm sure," Karl replied, "we approached that tree from the left, assuming that's west, we need to walk north of the tree. I laid my bag in that direction." Pointing, hopefully in the direction of the pub.

Karl and Claire walked for another half an hour, ignoring everything around them. The fog finally lifted, revealing the bright full moon in the dark sky above them. The couple could hear a faint howl in the distance, following them.

"Shit, we are no longer on the road."

"Did you hear that noise?" replied Claire, "let's keep walking!"

The weather suddenly changed, and as the rain started to fall on them, the pair moved quicker in the direction they hoped will bring them to their destination. Karl and Claire seemed to have been running for hours. Again, the howl was heard across the dales, and it was getting closer to them. The pair stopped so that Karl could move his torch in the hope of finding what was making the noise. Karl pointed his torch up to the sky just as the moon showed itself from behind the clouds.

"Shit, full moon!"

"Let's keep moving. I don't like this," said Claire, shaking.

"Over there," Karl replied, "a building, lights... thank fuck for that, the pub."

In the distance, about a mile across the dales, they could see, what looked like a light from a pub. Now closed for the night, a light glimmer in the dark, from a window.

"Come on, Claire, let's move!"

"I'm moving. Karl, I'm scared!"

"We just need to get to that building, and we will be safe. Come on."

Claire removed her shoes, and the couple ran towards the light, breathing heavily. They heard another howl, which stopped them in their tracks. Not knowing what was stalking them, they were shaking in their skins.

"That howl again, it's getting closer!"

"I'm scared," said Claire.

"Let's keep moving. It's probably just some dog lost out here," replied Karl, "we are nearly there."

They moved forward cautiously, not to make a noise and not to break a twig. Karl and Claire could sense something or someone circling them. This stopped them in their tracks, and Karl shouted into the night sky as he pulled his phone from his pocket.

"You're not funny... show yourself, or I'll call the police!"

There was no reply. Karl dialled the number and pressed send, "there's no signal!" he whispered to Claire.

Suddenly, Claire was dragged into the darkness, screaming for her life.

"CLAIRE!" Karl could hear her screams, "Where are you... Let her fucking go... Claire, I'm coming... Don't you fucking hurt her!"

Claire's screams turned to cries, and then the night became silent. Karl stumbled through the dark calling her name, but there was no response. He then saw her lying on the ground in front of him. Whispering her name as he moved closer to her, he then saw the devastation that had been done to her once-perfect body. Whatever had attacked Claire, it had ripped open her throat, and the flesh around her breasts had gone, showing her rib cage. Her eyes were still wide opened, and bloodshot, showing Claire's final seconds of fear. Karl knelt over her, caressed her blood-splattered face, and then he closed her eyes.

"What the fuck did this to you, my love!" he wept for her, and for his own safety. He had fallen for her, and now she was gone.

There was nothing he could do for her now, so he quickly retrieved his sleeping bag from his backpack and covered Claire's body. He pointed his torch towards the building, got up and ran for his life. He heard what sounded like the panting of a large dog following him. The noise was getting closer and closer to Karl. Suddenly, a swipe from the beast's claw took Karl's legs from beneath him and toppled him to the floor. As he laid on his back, Karl stared into the beast's empty green eyes, which had a bloodred tint to them. The werewolf stared back at him, and Karl called out for his brother.

"Brad!"

Meanwhile, back in London, Brad sat up in his bed shouting "Karl," then gasping for breath, he grabbed at his heart and fell back into the bed. Lucy was watching over him in the chair, next to his bed. She jumped to her feet to help Brad.

"Are you ok, Brad?" she called out as she pulled the emergency cord before tending to Brad. Brad mumbled to her, "there's something wrong with Karl!" before falling unconscious.

Dr Asker runs into the room, followed by the crash team and another nurse.

41

"He's unconscious, Doctor, possible heart attack!"

"Move, nurse, we need to act fast. There may be something we have missed from his accident?"

The team worked on Brad for about half an hour before bringing him back and stabilising his heart, but he is still unconscious.

"How is he, Dr Asker?" asked Nurse Lucy.

"He's alive but in a coma at the moment. The next few days are crucial. Lucy, some of the Doctors have been concerned about how close you have been getting to this patient," stated Dr Asker.

"I resent that remark, Dr Asker. I have been nothing but professional with this patient, as I am with any patient!"

"Hang on, Lucy, wait," replied the Doctor, "I know you have. You are an exceptional nurse... I think you should devote your time to him, just until a family member can come to his side. Maybe you can help him out of his coma... he knows your voice."

"Ok, Dr Asker, I can do that, sir."

"Thank you, Lucy. Do you think you can call his brother and his parents, and let them know what is happening?"

"Yes, Dr Asker, I will get straight on it."

"Thank you, Lucy," replied the doctor, "keep me informed on his progress?" the Doctor then walked out of the room as Lucy made the calls to Brad's family. First, she called Karl, "Straight to his voice message!" she said to herself before leaving a voice message.

"Hey, Karl, call me as soon as you get this message... it's about Brad. We have had complications... hate talking to these fucking things!"

Lucy then rang the brother's parents. She gave them the news about their son and tried to comfort them over the phone.

"I'll stay by your son's bed and talk to him to help with his recovery." She asked, "can you send me family details and memories that may help me with his recovery and pull him out of his coma?" She also told them that she had not been able to contact Karl.

"Why isn't Karl there with his brother?"

"Brad insisted that Karl continue with their travels. Brad was intending to catch up with Karl, once he was out of the hospital," said Lucy, "I thought they would have told you?"

"No," replied their father, "just like them to do that, and it's just like Karl to fuck off and leave his brother... Not the first time!"

Feeling awkward, Lucy assured the brother's parents, that she will look after their son. She will keep them posted on their son's progress. Lucy then finished her call.

"Thank you, Lucy... oh, she's gone?" as he turned to his wife and comforted her.

"Right, I'll give Karl a piece of my mind!" he called Karl.

"Mind what you say to him... you know Brad would have insisted that Karl goes on without him!"

Karl's phone rang as it laid in the mud underneath the full moon. Karl, alive and still holding his lit torch, looked up at the werewolf. With saliva dripping from her blood-stained mouth, the werewolf looked back at him. Karl was able to grab his phone from the mud just as the ring tone stopped. The beast, who towered over Karl at about eight feet tall, was a female. She was calm at the moment, but she could sense Karl's fear as he laid beneath her. She had already fed on Claire, so she was not hungry.

"Please don't hurt me!" Karl pleaded with her.

She was startled by the noise from Karl's phone, which he had concealed upon himself, as it rang again. She was also aware of the light from Karl's torch, which he dropped in the mud. She bit his leg and then dragged him away into an old derelict barn hidden by trees and overgrown with ivy and other wild plants. Once busied by agricultural work, the barn was now busied by the work of mother nature, and a great hiding place for one to do whatever deed they wanted to.

Meanwhile, from the top window of the Tan Hill Inn, where the light came from, stood Carol, the landlady.

"Honey, there's someone out there. I can see a light over there, across that field."

Her husband, Deryck, joined her at the window.

"Where?" he asked.

"Just left of that old barn, the light seems to have gone now," she surmised.

"You're seeing things again, darling. There's nothing out there," he laughed.

"Fuck off, there was something definitely out there!" She declared.

He replied, "I hope you don't kiss our grandkids with that mouth, dear... come on, let's get into bed. We must be up for breakfast at six... bloody guests to feed."

The pair settle in their bed, and Deryck lent over to turn the light out.

Deryck kissed Carol, "Night babe, love you!"

"Ditto," she replied.

As Deryck laid there in the dark, he wondered if Carol had seen anything on the dales?

"Did you really see something out there? Our guests are all back in tonight. The band are also in a room, didn't want to stay in their bus. Although their roadie is out there with his girlfriend."

"I'm sure I saw something out there!" explained Carol, "not all our guests are here, though. The two Americans who booked never turned up!"

To which Deryck answered with a snore.

"Oh, the prat's asleep… I wonder if that light was from those American lads?" Carol said to herself.

A father and his son were staying in a room on the same side of the building. It was Peter, and his son, Sean, who Karl had met on the train from London. Sean was looking out of the window, while his dad was in the bathroom.

"Dad, there is a light out there?"

"Why are you not in bed, Sean?"

"Dad come and look. There is a big dog out there. He's chasing that man."

Peter ran from the bathroom to his son's side, "where?"

"Over there, near that… oh, it has gone now dad."

"Are you lying to me, Sean?"

"No, daddy. There was a big dog out there. It was bigger than Scooby Doo, dad."

"There's nothing out there now. Come on, get into bed, we've got to go to nanny and grandads tomorrow. Come on, get under the covers. Give us a kiss, night, night."

"But, dad, there was one out there."

"Yes, ok. Go to sleep," Peter gave his son another kiss and turned the side light out, before climbing into his bed.

"Dad, I miss mummy!"

"I know Sean, so do I!"

"I love you, daddy!"

"I love you too, son. Night, go to sleep, son."

Chapter Five

One month later, at six o'clock on a Friday morning at the Tan Hill Inn, in December. The weather was terrible, it was as cold as a fridge, and had been snowing heavily. Thursday evening was not busy, but some of the weekend's guests had arrived early, to make the most of their cold weekend. Due to the weather, the staff stayed the night as well, insuring they would be at the pub for the long haul. Carol is in the bar with the chef, Tony, getting ready for breakfast.

"Cold out there, Carol. I think we're going to be getting more snow soon... I hope Max with our delivery gets here in time."

"Do we have enough food for the weekend? It's going to be a busy one, and I won't be surprised if we're not snowed in again, Tony!"

"There's enough for tonight, and possibly tomorrow," replied Tony, "big order coming today, but then so is that storm Alice... not good!"

"Here we go, Mr doom and gloom is in the room!" laughed Carol, "anyway, it's a snowstorm... when have they ever named a snowstorm?"

"Just saying! ... Storm Alice, named after my ex-wife and just as cold!" replied Tony.

"Tony, shut up. So, the storm has only been named by you? Alice was lovely... she just married the wrong bloke... can you give Max a call and find out what time he's getting here?"

47

"Thanks for that... I will call Max. What time are the band due?"

"They are here. Their tour bus is in the carpark. Their roadie's mobile home is with them too. I guess that girl is here again," said Carol as she opened a curtain and pointed it out to the bus.

"Oh, ok, cool."

"They'll want a breakfast this morning. I don't trust that girl who is with them. I'm sure I've seen her before?"

"She was with them last time, I think?" replied Tony.

"I know, but I'm sure that I have seen her before then?"

"Oh, ok. I have no idea about that. How many do we have for breakfast this morning, Carol?"

"There's the eight blokes from Norwich, here on a stag due."

Tony interrupts, laughing, "did they bring their sisters, I mean their wives?"

"Ha-ha, don't give up your day job, or maybe you should!" laughed Carol.

"How rude!"

"Anyway, there's an American and his English rose here as well, they are in room 10," replied Carol as she opened the curtains, "Oh, it's started to snow again... That's seventeen, no, sixteen, including the six in the band, but more are expected.... I guess it depends on this bloody weather!"

"Cool, I'll get started with breakfast... James and Sam are still asleep, I told them to join us at 7:30. Carol... where's Deryck? Is he still in bed?" enquired Tony as he walked into the kitchen.

"No, he's down the cellar, cleaning the lines and changing barrels," she replied as she started to set up the bar for breakfast.

A quarter of an hour later, Tony walked back into the restaurant, "Carol... I think we might be short of staff today, due to the snow. It's getting heavy out there. Trudy and Emily have both messaged, they can't get in."

"That's ok. I forgot to let you know that no one's coming down for breakfast until 8:30, we'll cope. We'll probably be short of customers this weekend as well. Not sure about the band, and when they want feeding, though!"

"What, that band staring through the window?" Tony points to the window.

"That's them!" came a voice from the cellar door as Deryck walked in and waved at the window, "morning Tony, morning sweetheart."

"Morning darling!" laughed Tony. "We have a full moon tonight!"... "Have you noticed that someone has gone missing every time this band has played here?"

"What are you running on about Tony? Mr doom and gloom fuck off back to the kitchen!" shouts Carol as she goes to let the band in, "morning boys, come in out of the cold!"... "What time did you arrive this morning?"

"We got here about two, Carol. We're starving!" said Jon, the lead singer and saxophonist.

"You ain't slept long?"

"I know, we were too hungry!" laughed the bass player, Gary.

"Ok, go through to the restaurant and grab a drink and some cereal," replied Carol, who then shouted, "no alcohol!" as the band walked into the restaurant.

"Morning lads... would you like four pints of line cleaner?" Deryck called from behind the bar as he pulled the line cleaner and water through, to clean the lines.

"Cheers, Deryck. What's the percentage?" laughs George, the rhythm guitarist.

Deryck raised his glass of line cleaner and water, "it will clear you out, and set you up for the day," laughed Deryck as he then tipped it down the sink and headed back to the cellar.

The band had two more members, Glenn, who played the drums, and George, rhythm guitar and keyboards. They had called themselves 'The Immature Graduates,' as they had just finished university as mature students. The band's choice of music was eighties Ska and two-tone, Madness and The Specials, amongst others. These were the bands they used to listen to when they were younger. One more member was their roadie Jack and his girlfriend, Tanya. Now, you already know Jack and Tanya. Jack had not been with the boys long, and he did not really fit this band as he looked more of a hard rocker, than a rude-boy or a mod. He was wearing double denim, long hair, and a beard, and he preferred heavy metal music. However, he did not look like Tanya's usual type of man either, as he was a lot shorter than her, and she was glamorously dressed in designer clothes. Since they first met, she had not been able to persuade Jack to change his appearance. Maybe, there was something else going on with this couple, about which we did not know?

Chatting to Carol, the band sat down, ready for breakfast. The roadie and his girlfriend sat on their own, away from the band.

"Does your roadie drive the bus?" asked Carol

"No, no one drives my bus!" replied Jon.

"He's a bit protective about his bus," laughed George, "Just like Cliff Richard in Summer Holiday."

"Piss off!" laughed Jon while the others laughed at him.

"No, Jack has got his own transport, a camper van," interrupted Glenn, "he and Tanya stay in that.

"Well, it's bigger than a camper van... it's one of those American style mobile homes, quite spacious inside. I think it actually belongs to her," said Gary.

"Nice... would you like four fry ups?" Carol asked

"Please, Carol," comes the thumbs up as Carol goes to the following table.

Carol took Jack's and Tanya's orders and then moved to the next table.

Tanya and Jack were whispering to each other, so that no one else could hear. Sometimes, blocking their mouths with their hands, as if concerned whether someone close by could lip read.

"It's a full moon this weekend. Will you two be ok?" Jack asked Tanya.

"We will be fine. Make sure you keep people away from your van," whispered Tanya, "make sure you do what he told you to do... we do not want any interference from the outside world."

"I will do my best... I'll need to find the phoneline and the Wi-Fi router first, so I can disable them," replied Jack, "But I need to do my job for the band as well, so as not to raise suspicion."

"If you want to live, you'll do better than your best!"

Meanwhile, Deryck was back down in the poorly lit cellar, moving empty barrels and cleaning the lines. With his back to the door, he felt uncomfortable, and he felt another presence in the room.

"Oh fuck, what is that?" he shivered and turned.

In the doorway were two dark figures hidden from the light. They moved forward to show themselves.

"You're not supposed to be down here, staff only!"

"Sorry, we followed you down here." Came an American voice, "I need some questions answered?"

"We are from room 10. I'm Lucy, and this is Brad," replied the female.

As they walked into the dim light, Deryck noticed the slight limp of the American.

"How can I help?" he asked as he sat down on a barrel.

"I was supposed to have been here about a month ago but never made it... the weekend of the last full moon."

"There's no need for you to have come and apologise!" smiled Deryck, "but welcome and thank you."

"No, you don't understand!" Brad explained, "my twin brother and I were booked in one of your rooms," Brad continued, "I was hit by a taxi when leaving Heathrow airport. I've only just got out of the hospital. Lucy here was my nurse."

"Hiya, nice to meet you," said Lucy as she shook Deryck's hand.

"My brother, Karl, came ahead to honour the room we had booked with you... No one has heard from him since. I'm trying to find out what happened to him!" a tear rolled down Brad's face, "did he arrive here? Have you seen him? We are identical twins."

Lucy then mentioned that "he was with a girl called Claire who was living in Richmond. She's missing as well."

"I haven't seen your brother; I don't recognise you... A police officer came. We could not answer his questions," replied Deryck, "I'm sorry for your loss!"

"Why do you say that? How do you know he's dead?"

"Calm down, Brad!" Lucy said as she squeezed his hand.

"Sorry young man, it was just a figure of speech!"

The three were disturbed, as they were suddenly joined by Deryck's wife.

"How come these guests are down here, Deryck?" Carol called as she walked into the cellar.

"This lad is one of the two Americans who never turned up last month, remember?" replied Deryck, "the lad who the police questioned us about, was the other one, his twin brother."

"We are sorry for your loss, but we can't help you!" explained Carol, "and if there was something living out there, we would know about it."

"Why do you people keep saying that? How do you know he's dead?" cried Brad. "What do you mean, if there was something living out there?"

"What's wrong with you people?" Lucy squeezed his hand again.

"Ok, I think you need to calm down and go upstairs!" declared Carol

"Come on, Brad, let's go upstairs and have breakfast." Lucy led him to the stairs and went back upstairs.

"Love, do you think that that light you saw that night could have been his brother?" whispered Deryck, "we should have told the officer."

"No, like you said that night, I was seeing things. None of our business!" explained Carol.

"But!"

"No buts! That's it, no more. Let's go upstairs, busy day ahead. We've got a busy weekend, too busy to worry about what happened a month ago," as the couple walked back upstairs.

All of the guests were sitting at their tables, being looked after by Sam. She had now come down for her shift, and James had joined Tony, in the kitchen. There were two unfamiliar faces seated at a table near the entrance. Carol headed straight over to them.

"Hiya guys, how are you? Have you booked into your room?"

"We haven't booked. We were hoping you had a room free?" said the young man, "don't fancy driving in that weather!"

"We only have one room left, it's a twin room, but we can push the beds together."

"That's ok. We are not a couple. We're best friends," replied the young woman.

"Ok, if one of you can come with me to reception so I can book you in and give you your keys," explained Carol.

The young woman followed Carol to the reception, complementing her on her pub as they walked.

"Here we go, room two. How many nights would you like to stay, madam?"

"I think a couple of nights will do... are your pods outside available for this time of year? Can we book one for a meal tonight?"

"We don't normally get people to ask this time of year, but yes, they are underfloor heated. You trying to swoon your friend?" smiled Carol.

The girl laughed, "my gran used to use that word about grandad... But no, I'm definitely not Mo's type. My name is Jess. We hope the sky will clear, so we can see the full moon and the stars."

"Oh, hopefully not... I mean, I don't think the sky will clear tonight... Your payments have gone through. Here are your keys Jess. You have the pod from seven o'clock until close if you like. Not sure about the weather, though. Looks though it's getting worse out there?"

"Thank you!" Jess heads back to the restaurant.

"We are here for two nights, Mo, and we are having dinner in one of those pods tonight... oh, breakfast, lovely!" Jess sat down.

"Sounds fun?" replied Mo, "hopefully, the sky will clear so we can see the full moon!"

"Yes, but that woman said hopefully not," answered Jess.

"Oh... miserable cow," laughed Mo.

While the guests were tucking into their breakfasts, the staff chatted and had their morning cuppa in the kitchen.

"Well done guys, great service," said Carol, "James, Sam, you slept well, you guys ok? I'm glad you stayed over last night. You know how I worry."

"It was bad enough driving here, yesterday. I had to sit next to him!" Sam laughed as she looked at James, "but seriously, them roads out there weren't good out there, yesterday. If it carries on, I can't see many more guests getting here for tonight. I can't see anyone leaving tomorrow either!"

"Fucking hell, now who's doom and gloom?" laughed Tony, "I hope Max gets through. If not, we will have limited food."

"We have plenty of booze!" said Deryck, "you are the only doom and gloom merchant around here... us being snowed in won't be the first time. It's normal for us, Sam."

"Shut up, Deryck. Tony, can you give Max a call for an update," snapped Carol, who is welcomed by the shrug of Deryck's shoulders.

Looking at the clock, which now said 10:00, Tony walked into his office to phone the delivery driver, Max, who Tony was good friends with.

"Hiya Max, how's it going? Where are you?"

"Tony, how's it going?" replied Max, "I'm now heading to Richmond with a delivery. I'm then heading to you!"

"Who's that in the background?"

"Sarah. She's keeping me company for the journey."

"Hiya Sarah, how's you?" shouted Tony.

"Hiya Tony, I'm ok, how are you?" came her reply.

"Fuck sake, right down my ear!" snapped Max.

"Sorry mate! What time do you think you will get here?

"Depending on the weather, this afternoon or in the morning," replied Max, "I'm close to my driving time, so I'll be parking up near you for the night."

"Cool, we'll catch up for a drink tonight if possible?"

"Great, catch you later!" then Max finished the call.

Tony then walked back into the kitchen, where Carol and James were still cleaning up after breakfast.

"Max will be with us this afternoon or in the morning. He will get as close as possible, then park up for the night."

"Why?" said James

"He's short on driving time, and he's got a drop in Richmond first," replied Tony, "he's got Sarah with him!"

"Oh lovely, I like her!" said Carol, "thanks, Tony, keep me posted!"

"I will."

Carol headed back into the bar to help Sam clear up, and she pumped into the couple from earlier.

"Oh, hello again… Jess and Mo," Carol paused as she tried to remember their names, "how were your breakfasts?"

"It was lovely, thank you!" replied Mo as he poured himself another coffee.

"Just having a cuppa before we have a look around your lovely pub," said Jess, "we're not in your way?"

"No, you are fine… hope Sam is looking after you?"

"Where is everyone else, Sam?"

"Back in their rooms, bands back in their bus!" said Sam.

"Is Deryck in the office?"

"Yes, think so."

Meanwhile, now in their room, Brad and Lucy were resting on the bed. Brad tried to phone his brother again, "still nothing, his phones dead… where are you, Karl? These people know something, I'm sure of it… they're not letting on, something isn't right."

"I got that feeling too, especially from that landlady!"

"If only I didn't get hit by that fucking taxi, everything would be ok, me and Karl would be together, damn this shit!" cried Brad.

"Oh, thanks for that, fuck me then… that shows you care!… maybe, you, both would be missing now if you hadn't had your accident," replied Lucy.

"Hang on, that's not what I meant… you're the best thing that's happened to me, I love you, but if it means having my brother here instead of you," Brad cried, "he's my brother, we've been inseparable for 24 years."

"I'm sorry, Brad, I didn't mean that. Of course, you would want your brother here," replied Lucy, cradling her new love, "just cannot imagine you not in my life, though."

The couple laid there holding each other on the bed and kissed as they looked at the snow-filled sky through the window.

"I don't think we will find anything out with the weather like this!" said Brad, "I think we are going to hit a dead end at every turn?"

"We should have gone to the café where that Claire worked to see if we could find anything out there?"

"Good idea. We will go there as soon as we have finished here," replied Brad, "we might be stuck here for a while, with this weather, though!"

"Let us have a look around this lovely pub, and then go and get pissed in the bar?" suggested Lucy, "take your mind off things!"

"Great idea, brains as well as beauty. That's why you drive me crazy, babe." As he looks out of the window, "that looks like fun, soccer in the snow!"

"What?"

"That bucks party, and the band are playing soccer over in that field. Shall we go and join them?" smiled Brad.

"Of course, we should... with your ankle?" replied Lucy, "and it's a stag party, and they are playing football."

"Whatever!" Brad shrugged his shoulders, "let's go and watch."

"Ok!"

Brad and Lucy got dressed for the weather and went downstairs to join them outside. The pair stood near the band's bus and the roadie's motor home, which felt like a good windbreak. Unfortunately, it was no protection from the snow. They stood there for about fifteen minutes when Brad pulled his phone out.

"Who are you calling?" asked Lucy.

"Just going to give Karl a call… see if he answers."

"Ok…"

Brad phoned his brother, who had the same ringtone as him. They both had the star-spangled banner as their ringtones, quite distinguishable in England.

"Can you hear that… it sounds like my ringtone."

"All I can hear are my teeth chattering," replied Lucy as she headed back to the pub's warmth, "I'm going back inside, to get warm. It's too cold out here… see you in a bit."

"Ok…" said Brad as he turned to the bus and then to the motor home, still listening for the ringtone. He decided that what he thought he could hear was coming from the motorhome and looked through the back window. The curtains were drawn, and all Brad could see were a pair of very hairy feet. Brad's phone finally went silent, and he said to himself, "they can't be Karl's feet. His feet are not hairy like that… I must have been imagining things?"

He headed back into the pub to join Lucy, who was in the bar sitting near the fire, sipping on a cup of tea.

"It's too cold out there, babe. I must be going mad, I thought I heard Karl's phone out there."

"It must be because you have it on your mind, that you are just hearing things, sweetheart."

While Carol and Sam were sitting in reception, Carol looked up as a winter clad Deryck was heading outside.

"Where are you off to?... I hope you are not going to join the football game outside... with your back."

"No," laughed Deryck, "I'm going to take the tractor and plough up and down the road, clear the road, hopefully, make it easier for Max. I'll see if any lost customers are out there, who needs help."

The pub owned all-weather terrain vehicles in the carpark. A tractor with a snowplough, and a Hagglund all-terrain vehicle, a converted burger van for outside gigs at the pub in the summer. The music could be as loud as they liked, as there was no one else for miles to complain.

"Ok, sweetheart, be safe. How long will you be?"

"Hopefully, an hour or so, I'll go about half a mile that way," pointing to his left, "then I'll come back and do about half a mile towards Richmond," as Deryck pointed to his right. Deryck then headed into the storm for his tractor.

"Oh, your hero Carol!" smirked Sam.

"Shut up, Sam!" laughed Carol as the front door opened again, "that was quick, love."

Four girls, Charlotte, Chloe, Gina, and Lisa walked in from the cold, all in their mid to late twenties. The girls were from London, and worked in either banking or real estate, earning lots of money. They have known each over since school, concentrating on their careers instead of relationships. The girls worked hard, and they liked to play just as hard.

"I don't know? we've been on the road since eight this morning," said one of the girls who entered the pub.

"Ah, you must be our four from London, Charlotte?" replied Sam.

"Yes, only just made it through that storm. Nearly went back, but, hey-hoe," explained Charlotte.

"Who's the madman in the tractor?" replied Gina, "he nearly hit us!"

"He's my husband... I'm Carol. We are your hosts."

"He was hardly moving. It was your driving Gina!" muttered Lisa as they all laughed.

"Here's your keys. If you can just sign in?" Sam interrupted.

"Thanks!" replied the fourth girl, Chloe, "is the bar open yet?! ... I'm starving!"

"Follow me, it's midday, and I'm now opening the bar up," as Carol led the girls through to the bar, she asked, "your bags?"

"They are in the car," said Lisa, "we'll get them later."

"Can I get you, girls, a drink?"

"Four large glasses of pinot, please, Carol!" asked Charlotte, "and another bottle chilling."

Carol prepared the drinks and took them over to the girl's table. As she reached the table, the door opened, and three members of the stag party walked in from their game of football.

"Hello!" said the youngest to the girl's table. They sat at a table within the talking range of the girls and asked Carol if they could move two tables together for their friends still playing football outside.

"You can, but you'll have to move it yourself!"

Within seconds, the lads had joined the tables together and, removing their coats, sat down.

"Thank you, Carol. Three pints of your best ale, please?" asked Eddie, "we start at the weakest and go up the list to your strongest... probably stopping at your weakest, thanks!"

"You enjoyed your game of footy?" said Lisa, as she smiled at Justin.

"Yes, it was fun, bloody cold though," answered Justin. He smiled back, "too cold for the oldens. As their carer, I had to bring them in from the cold."

"Cheeky git... shut your face!" replied John, about five years older than Justin. However, all the stags are only between twenty-eight and thirty-five years old.

Over the next couple of hours, the bar filled up with the other guests already at the pub, giving the room a good vibe. The bar looked old, but not tired, with its stone floor, and old beams above, covered with badges of beers that the pub had sold in the past. Sitting at tables or the stone bar, customers had been fed, and the beer and wine were flowing as the snow fell outside. Sam re-joined Carol behind the bar.

"I've just let the band into the function room to set up. I've set the bar up as well."

"Thanks, Sam... Clare and Simon are on their way," replied Carol, "but no one else can make it in."

"Do you reckon, in this weather?"

"Simon can get anywhere in his land-rover!"

Suddenly, Deryck walked in with a young couple, who look wet and cold.

"Hiya darling, I found these two on my way back... they were heading towards Kirby Stephen, stuck in the snow."

"Your husband is our hero. We thought we were goners," replied the girl, "I'm Amber. This is my husband, Alex."

"Go and sit down. I'll bring you over some hot drinks and soup," said Carol as she went into the kitchen, "Sam, sort them out with a room," she shouted to Sam.

"Ok! We have had another cancelation. I'll put them in their room," shouted Sam as she headed to reception to retrieve the key for the young couple.

Sam popped into the office and started to talk to Deryck about the band.

"The band are now setting up in the function room, Deryck," said Sam. "Don't you think that roadie looks out of place with that band? I've seen him somewhere before?"

"Well, of course, he was with them before when they were last here."

"No, I'm sure I have seen him before then, and that woman!"

"Are you sure? I think you are getting muddled up with someone else?"

"Possible? Anyway, better get them keys for that couple you brought back. See you in a bit, Deryck," said Sam as she went back to the bar with the keys.

Chapter Six

Tony was in his kitchen with James, his commis chef, getting ready for the evening service. The two chefs were quite different in appearance. Tony was short, and quite plump, whilst his colleague was taller and athletic. There was a ten-year age gap between them, and they had been working together for the last three years. James was married to Mary, with a young family, two boys and a baby girl. Tony's children were a lot older, and he had just divorced their mother, Alice.

The time was three o'clock, and Tony had decided to give Max a call, to find out where he was with their delivery. The two had just finished lunchtime service and were now clearing up, ready for later. They would normally have someone else to help, but Tom, their pot wash, could not make it to work due to the weather.

"Hello Max, it's Tony. Where are you?"

"I'm about ten minutes away, run out of driving time," replied Max, "I'll hopefully see you in the morning?"

"Do you want Deryck to come and pick you up in the tractor?"

"No, can't leave the lorry, got your perishables in the back... got Sarah with me to keep me warm!"

"Ok, stay safe... What was that?" Tony asked.

"Don't know, maybe a sheepdog?... I can't really see anything out there. Oh, lost him. I seem to have lost the signal, Sarah. It's shit out here," said Max

"Max, Max? I've lost the signal, James!"

"Are they ok, Tony?" asked James.

"I think so. He has parked up for the night," explained Tony, "he's not far, but run out of driving time. You know what he's like for the rules... I heard a strange noise in the background. It sounded like a dog, howling... I'll just let Carol and Deryck know where max is."

"Ok. Before I carry on clearing up this mess, I'm just going for a smoke," replied James.

"Ok. I won't be long."

That evening, the band was going to play in the function room, which looked quite modern, with a stage and a bar. Deryck had gone through to talk to the band as they were doing their sound check for the evening.

"Are you all ready to start? Can you start early... Take the guest's mind off the weather, start in about two hours, about seven?" asked Deryck, "they are coming through for their dinner, so they'll probably be ready for some music at seven."

"Yes, we can start that early."

"Where's your roadie?" said Deryck.

"He went back to his girlfriend in their camper van ages ago. He's a rocker... he doesn't like our sort of music. He only helps us set up and then clear up afterwards," replied George.

"He's a weird one... How long has he been with you?"

"He joined us just before we played here last!"

"Ok, Sam seems to recognise him from before that, perhaps with another band," said Deryck, "anyway, I'll let you get ready, and I'll bring the guests through here at about 6:45."

"Cheers, Deryck."

Shortly after, Simon and Clare came through to set up, ready for to open the bar early. They had only just turned up, due to the harsh weather.

"Hiya guys, you made it in... thank you," said Deryck.

"Yes, only just... I'll jump on the bar straight away, and get set up for tonight, Deryck."

"Ok, cool, Simon. I'll head back into the main bar to see how they are getting on with dinner. See you in a bit," replied Deryck.

"Do you guys want any drinks?" Simon asked the band.

"Please, four pints of lager, mate!" replied Jon.

The band spends the next thirty minutes finishing their soundcheck while Simon and Clare dance from behind the bar. They then sat down for a break and enjoyed their drinks until it was time to start. Just as Simon took another tray of drinks to the band, the guests started to filter into the room.

"Hiya guys, hope you have been well fed. Get your drinks and make yourself comfortable, people. The band will be starting in a moment," Simon announced on a microphone from behind the bar, "I hope you like eighties ska music. I love it!"

"Tonight, we have for you four great guys, playing Ska and Mod covers and some of their own songs... give a warm welcome to tonight's band at the Tan Hill Inn, The Immature Graduates."

There came a loud cheer from the small crowd, as the band started to play their first song. A late seventies classic, Ghost Town by The Specials.

Some of the guests were missing from the function room. Brad and Lucy were still in the other room, sitting at the bar chatting with Sam. Mo and Jess were outside eating in the pod. The snow had stopped, and the clouds had cleared to show the night sky and the full moon. Mo was Egyptian, he had come to England as a student, and stayed after he had graduated. He was six feet tall, and due to all of his cycling; his legs were muscular. Jess was five feet tall, slim, and covered in tattoos. Their friendship had grown from working together.

"Wow, it's as if the sky has cleared just for us, Jess? How romantic, pity we're not lovers!"

Jess laughed, "fuck off, you prick, that would ruin this perfect night sky... it's only meant for friends, not for lovers!"

"You are right!" said Mo, "look at that full moon, beautiful!"

"That sheepdog is enjoying it. Listen to his howl," replied Jess, "how primitive."

"The Hound of the Baskervilles. All we need now is Holmes and Watson?"

Back inside the pub, Deryck had returned to the main bar to join Sam. Sam started to show pictures from her phone to Deryck whilst Brad and Lucy sat at the bar, listening in.

"There you go, Deryck, I knew I'd seen that roadie before," explained Sam, as she flicked through the pictures on her phone, "he was with that rock band who played here two months ago, on that full moon... That woman went missing that night!"

"Hang on, what was that? What did you say?" interrupted Brad, "when I asked you earlier, you said you knew nothing!"

"Just a coincidence. You know what these rockers are like. He probably ran off with a groupie?"

"Fuck you. I spoke with this band earlier, and they told me that they were here last full moon when my brother went missing. And now it turns out that the roadie has been here for the last three full moons. Just a coincidence, hey?"

"Where's the roadie now?" asked Lucy

"He's through there with the band, calm down," replied Sam.

"He's not!"

"You what, Deryck?"

"He's not through there. He went back to his van a couple of hours ago."

Carol and Tony came through from the reception, "Max will not be with us until the morning... he's out of driving time."

"Ok, want a drink Tony?" asked Deryck.

"Just a quick half, better get back to help James."

Meanwhile, back at the lorry, Max and Sarah were settling down for the evening. The couple, both in their thirties, had been together for four years. First blaming each other, and then comforting one another after their spouse's had ran off together. Being left with three young children between them, they helped each other, and this grew into a relationship. Sarah often joins Max on his deliveries, whilst her mum looked after the children. Whilst they were preparing their supper in the cab, their room for the night, they heard the howling from outside again.

"That howling is getting louder. It's getting closer. What the fuck is it?" said Sarah nervously, "that's no sheepdog! Ring the pub, get them to come and get us!"

"I can't leave the lorry with deliveries on board."

"You can't, but I fucking can!"

"Shush, I'll take a look out there, prove to you it's nothing to worry about. Pass me that cricket bat?"

"If it's nothing to worry about, why are you taking a fucking cricket bat? Stay here, don't go out there!"

"Don't worry, I won't be long. Lock the door behind me."

As Max climbed down from his cab, he switched his torch on. He vigilantly walked around his lorry, careful not to make a noise. Max could hear a noise as if something were stalking his every footstep. He moved about ten metres from the front of the lorry, searching from left to right in an arch with his torch. The noise Max could hear seemed to be getting louder, making him nervous. He turned to the truck, still holding his cricket bat in one hand and waved his torch. The light was on in the cab, and Sarah was frozen in her seat.

"Be careful!" she mouthed as she waved him back to the safety of the cab.

He points to his door, "I'm coming back. Unlock the door!"

He started to walk back towards the lorry, when suddenly, he was pounced upon, and pushed to the floor. A chilling scream echoed through the cab as Sarah watched her man from beneath the beast. Looking at her, Max mouthed back to her, "I love you!"

Max was a big and strong man, but that could not help him from beneath this monster. Seconds passed before the beast took a breath and then bit at Max's throat, ripping his windpipe out, and then tearing at his chest. The snow around Max turned red as he raised his hands and tried to grab the werewolf's throat. His arms slumped to the ground, as life left his body. A minute or two passed, when suddenly a second werewolf joined the beast. They both turned and looked straight at Sarah, still frozen, as she stared back at the beast. They prowled the front of the cab keeping their eyes on Sarah. They then turned their attention to Max's body, eating at some of his flesh. Determined not to meet the same fate as her lover, she stretched over to the steering wheel, turned the key, and switched on the hazard lights and the high beam, and then she pressed on the horn. With this, the beasts were startled, looking back at where the sound was coming from. They stared straight at Sarah, and then fled into the dark night, heading in the direction of the pub. Sarah was now alone in the cab. Although petrified, she felt a slight calmness wash over her as she climbed into the back of the cab, and coward under the duvet.

Back at the pub, Mo and Jess enjoyed their time in the pod, full of the food they had just eaten. Wrapped up warm, they are still enjoying the night sky.

"Let's go in, in a bit, see the band?" said Jess.

"You getting bored?" replied Mo

"No. Now we are stuck here. We might as well make the most of what they have to offer... We might be here for a few days!"

"Fair enough. We'll go in in about half an hour." As they cuddle up to keep warm.

"What's that noise? Sounds like a car horn?" said Mo.

"Look, it seems to be coming from that light over there!" answered Jess as she pointed towards the direction of the road and Max's lorry.

"I can hear that dog again. It seems to be getting louder too," said Mo, "it sounds like there maybe more than one dog out there, now."

"It's getting a bit creepy out here. I think it's time we went back inside," replied Jess.

"Yes, I agree."

From inside the pub, Deryck asked if anyone else could hear anything, as he stood near the window. Deryck was joined by Brad at the window, as they looked out, Mo and Jess waved to them. They both looked at the couple in the pod and then over to the light in the distance.

"Sounds like the horn from a truck!" explained Brad.

"That must be Max with our delivery... Are they in trouble?"

Meanwhile, while Carol and Tony were chatting at the bar, Tony's phone rang.

"Hang on, it's Max... Hiya mate, how's it going? Who's that, Sarah? Is that you? What's wrong, where's Max? I can hardly hear you, sweetheart. You keep breaking up... what's wrong?"

"He's dead, his body is outside, it's in pieces, Max is dead!" cried Sarah, "two large dog-like beasts killed him... Please help me, come, and get me. I'm scared. Please come and get me!"

"What did you say, Sarah?" replied Tony.

"Max is dead. He was attacked by something out there."

"What, fuck. Listen, Sarah, lock the doors and hide," explained Tony, "We will come and get you as soon as possible. Where are the creatures now?"

"I think they are heading in your direction. ... help me!" The phone then went silent.

Tony looked at Carol, "Lost the signal, it's Max, he's been attacked by some sort of beast... Sarah is all alone in the lorry!"

Carol asked if Max was dead. Tony nodded his head.

Carol called out, "we have a problem!"

"Shush!" said Deryck.

"It's stopped now. The horn has stopped!" explained Brad.

"Maybe they are ok?" replied Deryck.

"He's dead, he's dead," shouted Carol.

"What!?"

"Max has been killed by some madmen out there. Sarah is alone in that lorry," cried Carol, "we need to help the poor girl."

"Hang on, she never said madmen. She said some sort of dog-like beast," said Tony.

"Shut up, Tony!"

"Would that be the same beast that killed my brother and his friend?" shouted Brad.

"I thought you said they were missing!" answered Carol.

"Does it fucking matter, woman, under the present circumstances?" interrupted Lucy, "something's not right here. You are not telling the truth!"

"Wait," shouted Deryck as he pointed at a figure outside, "what is that out there? It's huge."

"It looks like a wolf. It's standing. It's heading towards those in that dome!" screamed Lucy, "the door looks as though it is still open."

"Bloody hell, they're wasting that heating. It cost us money," moaned Carol, as she shook her head in frustration, "some guests just don't give a shit!"

Everyone in the room turned and gave Carol a disapproving stare. Brad and Deryck turned their attention to the window, banging on the glass. They called out to get the couple from the pod's interest. The beast moved closer to the pod and then stared at the window. Brad and Deryck froze with terror as a second beast came into view. Both of the werewolves headed towards the open door of the pod. Brad and Deryck return to trying to warn Mo and Jess.

Mo's and Jess's attention was suddenly drawn to those in the pub, trying to warn the couple of their imminent danger.

"What's that noise?" Mo said as he turned in the direction of Brad and Deryck's voices.

"Shit!" Jess turned around just as the werewolves walked past the glass dome.

"Oh. That doesn't look good," whispered Mo.

"Oh fuck, what do we do?" she wept as the two cowered behind the table.

"Hopefully, they haven't seen us!" whispered Mo.

Both werewolves howled to their full moon before turning to the pod. As they stood at the door, they smelt the air as they sniffed out their next victims. They had heard and seen the couple, and more importantly, they had smelt the young adults. The two beasts joined Mo and Jess in the pod. The group stood at the pub's window and watched helplessly as the lights in the pod went out. Holding each other in fear, they could hear the frightening screams of the young couple. The lights flickered on and off a couple of times, which gave a glimpse of the horror inside as blood covered some of the glass. It was about fifteen minutes before the two beasts left the pod and headed off into the night, stopping to howl at their moon again. The moon suddenly shone a light over the blood-soaked pod, showing her children's lunar actions.

Those in the pub looked in horror at the pod, as it returned to darkness.

"Is there any way of them getting in this building? Are we safe in here?" shouted Lucy, in tears because of what she had just witnessed, knowing that there was nothing she could do for the couple as a nurse.

"Hopefully, we will be ok? All the doors are closed. I'll go and lock them all," said an anxious Deryck, trying to stay calm, "close all of the curtains!"

"I'll go and speak to Simon and Clare. Let them know what is going on," said a nervous Sam as she wiped the tears from her eyes.

"Make sure that the guests don't know, just for now," replied Deryck, "don't let anyone go out for a cigarette... hang on, I'll come with you."

Sam and Deryck left the bar to ensure that the pub was locked down and the rest of the guests were as safe as possible.

"Let's get these curtains closed!" said Carol, "look, it's started to snow again!"

"Look up at the sky. Them clouds are now covering the moon!" replied Tony, "we might be safe now that the moon is not visible to those beasts!"

"Hey, Tony, where's James?"

"He's in the kitchen, I'll go and let him know what's going on." Tony headed to the kitchen to check on his commis chef. Tony stood in the kitchen and called out.

"James, where are you?"

There was no reply, and then Tony noticed that the door leading outside the back of the kitchen was open.

"Fuck, he's gone out for a smoke!" Tony headed towards the open door, picking up a meat cleaver. Gingerly standing at the door, aware of what may be waiting for him, he turned on the outside light. Shocked by what he found outside; he dropped his weapon. In the blood-soaked snow, his friend laid, ripped to shreds with his innards laying around him, and the lit cigarette still in his mouth. Tony knelt next to James's body and talked to him, "I told you that smoking would kill you one day!"

Carol called from the kitchen, "Tony, James, get indoors, close that fucking door!"

Tony walked back into the kitchen and closed the door behind him.

"Where's James?"

"He's out there in the snow!"

"Get him in, you idiot!"

"Don't go out there, Carol. You won't like what you see… James is dead!"

"Oh fuck!" cried Carol as she looked at James's broken body and then turned to hold Tony.

"What are we going to do?"

"We need to go through to the music. All stay together as one group before we can get them to their rooms," explained Tony, "come on, Carol!"

Carol seemed calm earlier in the bar, considering what had already happened. Still, after seeing James's body, her emotions seemed to change for the worse.

Chapter Seven

The time was ten o'clock, and the band had been playing for three hours with no break. Everyone was watching the band, unaware of what had happened outside. The music was loud, and most of the guests were in front of the stage, dancing and enjoying themselves. Carol and Tony came in and joined the rest of the staff who sat at the bar. Brad and Lucy sat on their own at a table near the exit. Tony looked upset, but Carol looked stone-faced and emotionless as if all her feelings had been drained from her.

"Carol, Tony, what's wrong. Where is James?" asked Deryck.

"Are we all locked up now, Deryck?" Carol replied.

"Yes, but where's James?"

"He's gone!" Tony said, shaking his head, "what are we going to do? We are fucked, there's two of them out there, with four dead bodies, and Sarah is alone in that lorry, that's if she is still alive?"

Sam started to cry as Alex, the guest Deryck had found on the road, came to the bar. Simon comforted her, "calm down. We must not spook the others!"

"Hiya, can I have a pint and a large merlot, please?" Alex asked, "what's wrong?"

"Nothing to concern you!" said Carol.

"Carol… Sorry about my wife. We have had some sad news about a friend."

"Oh, sorry to hear that!... the band are good," replied Alex, looking in the direction of the stage. Not knowing what else to say, Alex headed back to the table where his young wife was sitting.

Once Alex was out of ears reach, those at the bar continued with their conversation

"I'm not happy with those two sitting over there. We need to keep a close eye on that couple and keep them quiet," snapped Carol, looking at Brad and Lucy.

"They are ok, Carol... they are just in shock," said Deryck, "don't forget, that lad lost his brother in the same way."

"How do we know that? ... they might be involved," replied Carol, "They are not here for the same reasons as everyone else. They know too much!"

"What are you on about, Carol? You are talking mad!" answered Tony, "It was his brother who went missing last full moon."

The group looked over at Brad and Lucy, who were also chatting while glancing over at the staff.

"What are those wankers talking about?" whispered Brad, "I guess they are talking about us. They are up to something!"

"We should call the police!" answered Lucy.

Looking at his phone, "I would if I had a signal!"

"There's a phone in our room. We could use that?" replied Lucy.

"Come on, let's go upstairs!"

Brad and Lucy headed for their room. All at the bar were watching them as they left. Alex had been observing everything and noticed the tension between the two groups.

"Something is wrong... there's a bit of tension over there," Alex said to his wife.

Meanwhile, Carol had lost control of her own mind after the death of James. She had grown suspicious of everyone, especially Brad and Lucy.

"Where the fuck, are they going? Perhaps they'll try and leave and get themselves killed!"

"Fucking hell Carol, you can be one evil cow sometimes," replied Deryck.

"Fuck off, my mum warned me about marrying you," snapped Carol,

"Pity she didn't warn me off you, too!"

"Hey, come on, you two, this isn't helping!" said Simon.

Carol picked up a bottle of whiskey, the ice bucket, and a glass. She headed to the table where Brad and Lucy were sitting and poured herself a drink.

"Forget about her!" replied Deryck.

Just then, the music stopped as the band got ready for their next song. Deryck noticed three of the guests walking over to the fire exit.

"What are those three up to?"

Tim, Paul, and John from the stag party opened the fire exit, and went outside for a smoke, pulling the door ajar behind them.

"Shit, stop them!" said Deryck.

"It's too late," whispered Tony, "hopefully, there's nothing out there now?"

The four waited nervously while the smokers were still outside. They were concerned of what may happen next.

"We need to call the police!" said Tony.

"We need the army!" replied Deryck.

"What about the two in that mobile home, the roadie and his girlfriend?" asked Simon.

The fire exit opened again, and the four watched nervously as the three smokers re-entered the room.

Simon called over to them, "close the door behind you!"

Paul, looking over, returned to the door, and closed it, making sure that it was locked. He turned and raised his thumb up to Simon and re-joined his friends.

"Thank fuck for that. I guess those werewolves need to see the moon to act, it must be still snowing, and the clouds are hiding the moon," explained Tony, "this is going to be a long night!"

"The two in the camper van?" interrupted Sam, as she flicked through the pictures on her phone, "I knew I'd seen her before!"

"Yes, she was here with him when the band were here last," replied Tony.

"Yes, and she was here when he was here with that other band back in October. She was the girl who went missing that night," explained Sam, as she showed them the image of the girl on her phone and then pulled out the picture that the police had left them, "it's her mobile home, not his."

"Phew, at least she is alive!" replied Simon

"Yes, but two people were killed a month later when those two were here."

"We don't know if they are dead!" came the response from Deryck.

"Are you really that blind, Deryck," said Sam, "we have four dead bodies out there, and where are those two?"

"Sam, what are you getting at?"

"Deryck, Sam has a good point there... we cannot ignore this fact," replied Simon.

"Ok, ok!" said Deryck, "look, we need to keep everyone in tonight. We have a few rooms empty... Sam sought out some keys for the band. They'll be finishing soon... we need to stick together and get through the night and survive till the morning. We'll keep the bar open till everyone has gone to bed."

"Ok, I'll get some keys," replied Sam.

"Tony, call Sarah, make sure she is ok. We will get her tomorrow!"

"Ok, Deryck!"

"Simon, keep them drinking in here!"

"Ok!"

"What's going on?" asked Clare as she returned from watching the band whilst collecting glasses.

She stood in shock as they explained to her what had happened, and the death of James. She starts to cry.

"We must not fall apart like my loving bitch of a wife," replied Deryck, as he comforted Clare, "I'll go to my office and call the police."

The three left to do their tasks whilst Simon and Clare stayed at the bar.

Alex had been watching the bar since he got his drinks, "something is going on with that lot. They are being shifty!" explained Alex to his wife, as he played on his phone.

"That's the second time you have said that. What do you mean, honey?" replied Amber.

"Ever since they came into the room, they were staring and talking about that American and his woman. That landlady has been sitting on her own getting pissed," stated

Alex, "something is going on. Where's that couple who ate in the pod outside? They haven't been in here all night?"

"Maybe they went straight to their room, after their dinner?"

"Maybe, but it looks a bit suss to me!"

"Oh, you are just like your detective uncle," said Amber.

"I've messaged him!"

"What!... that's a bit over the top! How did you get a signal?"

"It sent. I think!" replied Alex as he put his phone down, "I'm sure that there is definitely something going on here... let's go to our room!"

As the couple left the room, they passed Deryck on his return. He nodded to the couple, asking them nervously if they had enjoyed their evening. With a suspicious look, Alex replied, "yes," and the two then headed for their room.

"See... didn't he sound a bit nervous to you?" said Alex.

"He did seem a bit strange... maybe you are right, darling," replied Amber.

Deryck returned to the bar. He whispered to Simon, "just been to the office, someone had been in there... the phone lines been cut, and the Wi-Fi router has been smashed."

"Fuck... that means we are all alone!" said Simon, "hang on, don't you still have that old router."

"Yes, I do... See what we can do tomorrow, don't tell anyone else!" explained Deryck.

It's about 11:30 when the band are finally finishing off their set. They finish with a cover of the Creedence Clearwater Revival song, 'Bad Moon Rising.'

Simon said to Clare, "If only they knew how appropriate that song is."

Despite what had happened, there was a good vibe in the room. Those still in the room, the band and the guests were unaware of what had happened outside on that cold winters night or what may confront them this weekend at The Tan Hill Inn. The band had finished and sat at the bar, talking to Simon and Clare. Tim and Paul from the stag party were sitting with them. Everyone else was seated at tables, drinking, and laughing. If they only knew what was going on around them. The band has left some background music playing. Two of the stags, Justin and Nev, were talking to a couple of the girls, Lisa, and Gina. A slow song started to play, and Justin took Lisa's hand for a dance, and she accepted. The pair walked to the dance floor, and started moving to the music, holding each other.

Brad and Lucy were now in their room. Brad was on the phone, trying to call the police. He was unable to get through, someone had cut the line.

"The line is dead, there is nothing, we are stuck, we are fucked!" whispered Brad.

"There's no signal either!" replied Lucy, "that chef said we should be safe with the clouds covering the moon... Do you reckon he is correct?"

"I don't know, but how can these people know such details but know nothing of what happened a month ago with Karl and Claire?"

"What if we cannot get out of here tomorrow? It's a full moon again tomorrow night." stated Lucy, "those poor people have no idea what is coming tomorrow night!"

Suddenly, there was a knock on their door. The two looked at each other nervously.

"Who's that?" Whispered Lucy, "you don't think that the...?"

"I don't think that the werewolves in Yorkshire are that polite, that they knock on doors," replied Brad as he headed to the door.

He opened the door to find Alex and Amber in the hallway.

"Can we talk?" asked Alex as he held a bottle of wine.

Brad looked over to Lucy, "come in!"

"Aren't you the couple who the landlord found stuck in the snow?" said Lucy.

"Yes, we were on our way to Alex's parents in Kirby Stephen when we skidded off the road," replied Amber, "If it hadn't been for Deryck, we would have been fucked."

Alex interrupted, "What's going on here?"

"What do you mean?" replied Brad as he shrugged his shoulders.

"I was watching you two, and those staff since you all came into that room," said Alex, "you were staring, and talking about them, and they were glaring at you as they talked about you, too. That's what I mean!"

"Oh, it's nothing!"

"I overheard the young waitress crying and talking about someone dead. They tried to fob me off with a text message of a friend who had died," explained Alex, "and that other couple, Mo and Jess... they haven't been seen all night, and all the doors downstairs are locked and bolted, and the curtains are closed."

"Don't mind him. He's like his uncle, a police detective," said Amber.

Brad starts, "Maybe that's how they lock...."

Lucy interrupted, "Brad, tell them the truth, or I will!"

Brad looked at Lucy, "But... ok!" and then he turned to the other two, "Alex, you are right. There is something going on, there has been for the last three full moons, including this one, and there is more to come."

"What do you mean?" replied both Alex and Amber.

"Two months ago, a young woman went missing out there," Brad said as he looked towards the window, "last month...."

Brad gulped with a tear in his eye while Lucy held his hand, "...last month my brother, who came to England with me, went missing... I was in a London hospital, and I persuaded him to continue with our travels."

Lucy spoke whilst Brad got upset, "Brad was supposed to meet up here with Karl, but Karl never made it here. He went missing, out there on the dales with a girl he met in Richmond. They were last seen by the driver, getting off the bus at a village called Keld, which is about four miles south of this place."

"Those people knew something but brushed it under the rug!" snapped Brad, "and now it's happening again... There is something out there, and we are stuck here with them!"

"I'm sorry to hear about your brother, but what do you mean?" asked Alex

"Mo and Jess, they are not missing. They are outside in that pod, both dead."

"What?" Amber cried.

"There is a lorry down the road, the driver is dead, and his friend is stuck in the cab!"

"What are you talking about, Brad?"

"There are two werewolf-like creatures out there. We watched as they killed Mo and Jess and started to eat them," explained Brad, "this happened whilst the snow had stopped, and the sky was clear... When the storm started again, they fled away from the pub. Or at least we think so?"

"The chef seems to think that whilst the clouds cover the full moon, they are not so active, and we are safe," said Lucy.

"You are talking about werewolves. This is Yorkshire, not Hollywood."

"Yes, and what we saw was real, not Hollywood," replied a frustrated Brad, "I don't know what they are out there. All I know is that they are dangerous, and we are not safe!"

"You can't see anything out there with all that snow!" explained Amber as she looked out of the window.

"Then hopefully, the chef is correct!" said Lucy

"I knew something wasn't right. I messaged my uncle, he's a police detective," declared Alex, "there is no reply yet, though. I don't know whether he got it!"

"The phone lines are down... and I don't think English cops will do much to them with their little batons," smirked Brad.

"Well, I don't see you doing much!" angrily snapped Alex, "come on, Amber, let's go and try and sleep. I'm tired."

Alex picked up the bottle of wine, and left the room, followed by Amber.

"I don't think that was called for, Brad. At least he is on our side!" said Lucy, "I'm off to bed too."

"Sorry, sorry, I'll apologise to them at breakfast!"

"If we make it till then!" replied Lucy.

Chapter Eight

The following morning, Brad awoke and just gazed at the ceiling, looking at nothing. He then looked at his phone.

"Ten o'clock, I slept quite well, considering. A bit of a hangover, though," he said.

"What's that?" answered Lucy.

"Oh, nothing... you're awake? Are you ok, babe? How did you sleep?" as he leaned over and kissed Lucy.

"I slept quite well, considering," replied Lucy, kissing him back, "how about you?"

"Me too... I wonder how today is going to go. It is going to be interesting at breakfast with them wanker's downstairs!"

"Who?"

"Lucy, I'm on about the staff."

"I guess they are just scared, scared of what's happened and what this means for their business," replied Lucy.

"A little goldmine if they work it right," explained Brad, "a couple of werewolf heads hanging over the fire. Tourists would travel for miles... they'll profit out of other's misery!"

"How sick, they wouldn't do that."

"She would, bitch!" retorted Brad as he got out of bed and headed for the window.

He opened the curtains and stood naked, looking across the snow-filled dales. Brad opened the window to let in some fresh air.

"It's still snowing... it is getting deep out there. We won't be going anywhere today."

"I guess we better go down for breakfast then?" replied Lucy as she headed for the bathroom, "join me for a shower, big boy?"

"Yeh, I'll be in in a bit," he replied, still staring out of the window. He noticed that the roadie's van was moving on the road, heading west.

"Where are they going?"

"WHAT?" shouted Lucy from the shower.

"Who's that?" he muttered to himself as he looked at a face in the van's window, "Karl, it can't be?" Brad stepped back, shocked at what he thought he saw.

"What, dear?" Lucy shouted again.

Brad looked again at the van's window, but the face had gone. Brad then received a wolf whistle from the band, who stood outside, smoking. He waved and then closed the curtains.

"What did you say?" Lucy shouted again.

"Nothing, I must be seeing things... I'm going mad!" Brad declared. He then joined Lucy in the bathroom. "Just seen the roadies van leave or trying to..." said Brad.

"Oh... hopefully, we will be safe today... come on, get in this shower. I'm feeling horny!" allured Lucy.

Once dressed, the two went downstairs to see what confronted them in the restaurant. This morning breakfast was running late, due to the night before. Had everyone been told about what had happened outside the night before, or were they all still clueless?

"Maybe the werewolves got in, and everyone is dead?"

"Brad!"

"Alright, maybe just the staff?"

"Brad, you're sick!"

"Ok, just the Landlady."

"Ok, that's better, yes, just the bitch!" laughed Lucy as they walked past the reception where the 'bitch' was sitting. She looked terrible, with a hangover. The two sheepishly said morning to Carol, smiling as they walked past her, trying not to laugh. Carol ignored them as they headed for the door to the bar. The two walked over to the table where Alex and Amber were sitting. Brad put his hand out, to apologise for how he had acted the night before.

"I'm sorry about last night, bro. I was out of order!"

Alex shook his hand, "that's ok, mate, sit down and join us."

"What have we missed?" asked Brad as the two sat down.

"We just passed the landlady at the reception; she doesn't look good," replied Lucy.

"Nothing has been announced yet, other than about the stranded lorry half a mile away," answered Alex, "the landlord has taken the tractor and two guests to fetch the lorry."

"Two of the guests?"

"Two from the stag party went with him," replied Alex.

Brad gets up and heads over to the stag party.

"Brad!" whispered Lucy.

He looked around but continued walking over to the stags table. He sat and talked to them for five minutes, and then walked over to the band's table.

"Hiya guys, great music last night."

"Thanks!" replied Glenn, "great exhibition this morning."

"Your roadie's camper van, are there three people staying in there?" asked Brad.

"Three people, I think not!" replied Jon.

"Are you sure?"

"Yes, I'm sure. I think we would notice if there was a third person in there."

"Ok, just thought I would ask... oh, by the way, he's gone," Brad replied as he headed back to his own table.

Once Brad was back at his table, he told the others what had been discussed with the stag's.

"One of those guys is a bus driver, and the other is a mechanic. He's hoping they can bring the lorry back here as soon as possible," explained Brad, "other than that, they know nothing."

"Did you tell them anything?" asked Lucy

"No!" replied Brad

"Something needs to be said," said Alex, "we can't let these people spend the day not knowing what may confront them tonight."

As the four were chatting, Sam came over to take their order for breakfast. Brad looked out of the window. He had to peak through a closed curtain. All of the curtains were still drawn from the night before.

"What would you guys like for breakfast? We are limited on food, though. All of our food is on the lorry down the road."

"How can you take breakfast orders knowing that that poor couple is lying dead?" enquired Alex, "you need to tell them what happened last night!"

"How do you know about last night?" replied Sam as she stared at Brad and Lucy.

"Don't blame us... Alex guessed that there was something wrong, so we told him," explained Lucy, "and we should also be telling the rest of the guests."

"It's gone, and so are they!" said Brad from behind the curtains.

"What do you mean?" asked Alex

"Their bodies are not in the pod, and that roadie and his camper van have gone... saw him drive away this morning", comes the reply from Brad, "seems suspicious to me... you think there's a connection?"

Sam explained to the group that Deryck and Tony moved the bodies first thing this morning, putting them with James's body, so no one could see them.

"I have no idea about the van. How the hell did it move in this weather?" said Sam.

"Hang on, who's James?" asked Amber.

"One of our other chefs who was working last night. Tony, the head chef, found his body in the courtyard at the back of the kitchen last night. They got him as well," said Sam as she started to cry, "he's got three young children!"

"Sit down, Sam!" replied Lucy as she held her hand.

"You didn't' have a lot of staff on last night?" asked Alex.

"Lucky for them... they couldn't get in through the snow," said Simon as he approached the table, "Tony and I have decided to tell everyone about last night after breakfast. Hopefully, the others are back by then. I've fitted our old router... you should be able to get signals on your phones now."

"What about Carol, Simon?" asked Sam

"Leave her in reception, she has lost the plot!"

Jon interrupted them, "what do you mean about Jack?"

"What are you on about?" asked Alex.

"He said that Jack had gone!" replied Jon, pointing at Brad.

"I saw him driving up the road this morning from my room... that's when I thought I saw a third person in the van," answered Brad, "what do you guys know about that couple?"

"We have only known them since he joined us about six weeks ago... he met that girl last time he was here with a different band... it's her van," replied Jon, "he's a weird bloke, got a couple of those Samurai swords hanging up in that van."

"The Katana and the Wakizashi," said Alex, "the Wakizashi was the blade associated with seppuku."

"Seppuku who?" asked Lucy.

"Ritual suicide," replied Alex as he drew his thumbnail along his stomach, "you probably know it as Hara-kiri. The Samurai committing seppuku will slice open his stomach from side to side."

"Alex knows his shit," said Amber as she watched her husband lovingly.

"Oh, are those ornamental ones?" answered Lucy.

"No, real ones... they are well sharp... he is often playing with them, he caught a rabbit the other day... Jack sliced it in half as he let it go," explained Jon as he walked back to his table.

"Fucking hell, what a wanker," snapped Lucy.

For the next hour or so, everything went on as usual. Everyone was chatting away as the guests enjoyed their food and planned their day stuck at the pub. However, Brad's table, who were not so positive, was waiting on tenterhooks for Tony and Simon's announcement about the horrific activities the night before.

Sean Watson

Chapter Nine

Meanwhile, out on the road, Deryck's tractor approached the stranded lorry. Deryck and his two passengers could see the truck through the snow.

"it seems so calm over there!" said Tim, the stag who was getting married.

"I can't see Max's body!" Deryck whispered to himself.

"What was that Deryck?"

"What? Oh, nothing."

"What the fuck is that!" shouted Justin, Tim's best man, pointing to the mound of snow being pushed in front of the plough. A hand, and then a bloody face became visible from the snow.

"Fuck... Max, there you are!"

"Who is Max?" replied Tim.

"I guess this is a suitable time to explain what's going on," explained Deryck, "this is Max. He is the driver of that lorry with our food on it... Last night... madmen or werewolves attacked us while you were listening to the music. Max was killed, and so was one of our chefs, James. Also, Mo and Jess, the young couple who were out in one of our pods."

"Who did you say killed them?" asked Tim.

"Madmen!"

"No, the other one you said. Werewolves!"

"Well, it was a full moon last night!" explained Deryck, "we haven't got time for this. I'll explain when we get back... Sarah!" Deryck looked at the lorry cab.

"Who?" inquired Justin.

Deryck pointed to the lorry, "Max's girlfriend, Sarah."

Sarah sat in the front, she was in shock, crying as she watched the tractor uncover Max's mutilated body from the snow.

"Max's girlfriend, she has been stuck here all night. We need to get her back to safety!"

"Somehow, I don't think you can class your pub as a place of safety, do you?" explained Justin.

"Ok, a point noted. However, it is safer than out here!" replied Deryck, "we need to work fast. Tim, go and make sure that Sarah is ok. Justin, we need to clear the snow from the front of the lorry. It's now 11:30... we must be back before 3 O'clock. The moon will be visible this time of year by then if this storm clears."

Deryck and Justin started moving the rest of the snow to the side of the road, so that the lorry was clear. They gently moved Max's body to the side of the road, making sure that he was covered. They finish off with a couple of shovels that Deryck has on his tractor.

"That should do!" stated Deryck. As he turned around, Sarah fell into his arms.

"Deryck, my poor Max," cried Sarah, "thank you for coming for me. What are we going to do...? How are we going to kill these creatures? We need to get out of here before we are attacked... they are everywhere?... What are we going to do?"

"Calm down, Sarah. First, we need to get you back to the safety of the pub, sweetheart!" said Deryck as he comforted Sarah, "get back in the cab. We need to get the lorry back for the food onboard... Tim, get in the cab with Sarah, and start the lorry."

"Ok, Sarah, you have the keys?" asked Tim.

"They are in the lorry," wept Sarah, still scared.

"Tim, take this!" Deryck said as he gave Tim a walkie talkie.

"Come on, let's get out of the cold!" the pair climbed into the lorry.

"Come on, Justin, let's get this lorry roped up to the tractor," Deryck said.

"Do you think that will hold?" enquired Justin, looking at the rope in Deryck's hands.

"It'll have to do!" Deryck replied.

Deryck and Justin tied the rope, getting a few lengths between the two vehicles to make it as strong as possible.

In the cab, Tim tried to get himself comfortable. He turned to Sarah and said, "Here we go!" as he turned the key, nothing happened. Tim turned the key a second time, again nothing. He looked to Sarah and then the two outside, shrugging his shoulders. He tried for the third time.

"for fuck sake, come on!" under his breath, he turned the key again, and... the lorry started.

"Yes!" came a relieved voice.

"Phew. Thank fuck for that," Deryck said to Justin as they climbed onto the tractor. Deryck started the tractor and began to move forward. Tim lifted his foot to release the handbrake as the rope stretched, dis-engaged the airbrakes, and pressed the accelerator. The vehicles started to move forward slowly, but suddenly the rope snapped.

"Fuck, the lorry is too heavy, Deryck! ... We'll have to lose the trailer?"

"We can't. We need the food."

"We can load enough food for today into the cab and come back for the rest tomorrow!" replied Justin, "the food should be ok in this weather."

Deryck thinks for a second.

"Deryck?"

"Ok, come on, let's do this!" replied Deryck. "We don't have much time, only an hour at most."

Deryck and Justin climbed down from the tractor and signalled the other two from the cab. Tim and Sarah joined them and were told what needed to be done.

Justin started to check the rope and re-connect the two vehicles. The other three went to the back of the lorry and opened the doors to reveal its contents. Deryck climbed on board and started to pass the food boxes to the other two. He moved the food to the back of the trailer whilst Tim and Sarah placed the boxes into the cab.

"We have fresh and frozen food on here," explained Deryck. "Make sure we take the fresh and some frozen. We can leave the rest of the frozen until tomorrow."

Justin joined them at the back of the lorry.

"I've sorted the rope. It should hopefully hold now once we disconnect the trailer."

"Great, take this!" Tim passed Justin a box and then jumped up to help Deryck.

"We need to disconnect the trailer!"

"We can do that once we have finished here," explained Tim as he moved some boxes to the back truck.

"That should be enough for now. Let's load these up," said Deryck as he climbed down.

"One more!" Tim shouted as he grabbed a box full of a selection of spirits. Not anticipating the distance of the ground through the snow, Tim jumped down and landed awkwardly. As he hit the ground, he twisted his ankle.

"Ouch... fuck, that hurt that did."

He got up and tried to walk on his injured foot, "shit, I can't stand on that foot. It hurts too much. I'm not going to be able to drive. Sorry, guys."

"You ok to sit with me in the tractor?"

"Should be, with this bottle of vodka as pain relief!"

"Ok, Justin, you'll have to drive!" explained Deryck, "Tim, can you give Justin a hand to disconnect the trailer while Sarah and I will finish up, here?"

"Will do... give me a hand Justin," Tim hobbled to the front of the trailer, helped by his best man.

"Deryck, look!" said Sarah as she pointed to the sky.

They had all been so busy with what they had been doing that they had not noticed the weather. It had stopped snowing, and the clouds were clearing from the sky.

"Come on, we better hurry up," shouted Deryck, "it won't take long to get dark up here! This will have to do. Sarah, leave the rest."

Deryck headed back to the tractor, followed by Tim, hobbling on one leg, and swigging at the vodka. Sarah climbed into the cab, taking a last look at the pile of snow where Max was lying. Justin joined her in the driver's seat. Deryck turned and gave Justin a thumbs up, with which Justin replied with his thumb, and started his engine.

"How's your foot, Tim?" enquired Deryck

"It's ok... this vodka is helping!"

"Hold on!" replied Deryck as he started the engine.

The tractor started to move forward, and the rope was stretched to its limit.

"Slow, Deryck, slow!" said a cautious Tim.

The lorry's cab started to move, and the rope held as they moved a little bit faster.

"The rope is holding, Deryck... it's working!" Tim shouted, pushing his fist to the sky, and then giving a thumbs up to the pair in the cab. The two vehicles were now moving at a steady pace. The plough pushed the snow away that had settled in front of them. It was now 3 O'clock, and the sky was beginning to get dark. They should be back at the pub within the hour at this pace.

"Please let us get back safely... I'll never fight with Carol again!" Deryck said to himself as he looked up to the sky.

"What?" replied Tim.

"Nothing," Deryck shook his head.

"Look!" said Tim as he spotted the pub in the distance, "we can do this!"

Meanwhile, back at the pub, everyone was still in the restaurant. Brad and Alex were looking through the window from behind the curtains.

"Alex, have you heard from your Uncle yet?"

"Yes, he said that he and his partner, Detective Longland, will get to us as soon as possible."

"How the hell are they going to manage that in this weather?" asked Brad, "just the two of them?... they'll need back up out there... and guns!"

"As detectives, they have firearms... Uncle Paul has a brother, Uncle Ruby, who drives a road gritter with a snowplough. He will bring them here," explained Alex, "I messaged him not to come without the full force of the law, as it's much too dangerous than I first thought. But I think he will ignore that message."

"What sort of name is Ruby?" asked Brad, "that's a women's name."

"That's a nickname. Don't you have nicknames in America?" snapped Alex, "call him a woman, and he's likely to thump you."

"Ok, I was only joking, Alex, but why Ruby?"

"You'll know why when you see his face," explained Alex, "I'm not sure that my uncle got my last message, or he's ignoring it... as detectives, them two are a bit gung-ho... a bit like you Americans. I'm worried that they'll come on their own."

As Brad's table were quietly talking, Tony was telling the other guests about what had happened the night before, and the situation that they were all now in.

"So, that's what happened last night, while the music was playing," explained Tony to everyone, "we lost four people last night. We need to be vigilant tonight! ... any questions?"

"Yes, just one," shouted Glenn, "why the fuck are we still here? We could have got everyone on our bus and followed that tractor out of here!"

"Yes!" replied Gary, "instead, they have gone to get food for our last supper!"

"They have gone to save a girl stuck in that lorry. She has already watched as these beasts killed her partner," interrupted Simon, "and it looks like your roadie is to blame for this!"

"Our friends are risking their lives to save her and bring her back here," shouted Paul, one of the stags, "when we could have picked her up on our way out of here!"

"Yes, and if we had got stuck out in that weather out there, we would have been more vulnerable than in here," replied Tony, "If the storm clouds hide the moon, we should be safe... we noticed that this was the case last night."

Brad shouted, "it has stopped snowing, and the sky has cleared... I can see the full moon!"

"They are coming!" declared Alex as some of the guests screamed, "No, I mean the landlord...I can see the tractor and the lorry moving slowly towards us... there is no trailer, though."

The screams suddenly changed to cheers and then silence as Jon laughed, "Oh well, no last supper!"

"Wait!" said Brad, "look, howling at the moon on the horizon. There are the two werewolves, standing up there."

"Fuck, those creatures are back!" shouted Alex.

"Fuck, those things are big," said Gary.

"How are we going to kill them?" asked Tony, "does anyone know anything about these creatures?"

"Yes, cos we have loads of these things back home," replied a sarcastic Brad.

"Ok, only asking!"

"What about garlic?" someone shouted.

"That's vampires. Idiot!"

"Isn't silver and wolfsbane affective against werewolves?" asked Sam, "works in the films."

"Pity we are not in the films," someone else shouted.

"Ok. Does anyone have any silver or wolfsbane?" said Tony.

"No!"

"No!"

"A silver-plated watch."

"What about your cutlery?"

"Stainless steel," replied Clare.

"Ok, we are pretty fucked then," replied Tony.

Back in the tractor, Tim had also seen what was on the horizon.

"Deryck, look up there!"

"Shit, let them know," replied Deryck as he passed the walkie talkie to Tim.

"Shit"

"Please don't tell me you still have the other one?"

"Sorry, Deryck, I forgot to give it to Justin," said Tim as he pulled the other walkie talkie from his coat pocket.

"For fuck sake!"

"Sorry! Look, we're going slow enough. I'll climb down and pass it through their window."

"No, it's too late now... try and get him on your mobile... hopefully, there's a signal," replied Deryck, "See that window on the side of the pub? I'll pull the cab to that window... it's about the same level as the cab. We can get in through there. We could also pass the food through the window."

Tim managed to get through to Justin and put him on his phone's loudspeaker, "Cool, say all that again, Deryck."

Deryck repeated himself so that Justin and Sarah could hear his plan.

"Did you hear that, Justin?" asked Tim.

"Yes, you sure this will work?" replied Justin

"It has to," said Deryck.

Deryck then retrieved his phone and called Tony, so he could relay his plans to those in the pub.

"Tony, listen carefully... I'm going to park the cab outside the window on the stairs," explained Deryck, "get ready to get us in, and the boxes of food that we have with us... Also, get people to help barricade the front doors, use tables and chairs... Barricade all doors, make sure nothing is getting in!"

"Ok, boss... how is Sarah?"

"She's ok, upset though... How's Carol?"

"Not good. She hasn't left reception... Carol's just sitting there drinking, oblivious of everything and everyone!"

"Ok, thanks, Tony!"

"Deryck... we have told everyone what is going on."

"Ok, cool... they needed to know," replied Deryck, "It will make it easier for you when you ask them to help you with what you need to do... See you on the other side!"

"We'll be waiting for you... Stay safe, mate!" as they finished their call.

Tony quickly organised teams to go and block all the doors on the ground floor. Simon took the girls from London, through to the function room to block the doors in there. Claire and Sam went through to the kitchen, to block the back door, from those outside. The rest in the bar, made sure that the porch entrance was blocked, before taking tables through, to block the main entrance later. Within half an hour, everyone was back in the bar. Simon and three of the

Sean Watson

guests went to the stairs to help Deryck and the others in, whilst the doors were bolted behind them.

The air was suddenly filled with the sound of howling. Tim grabbed Deryck's arm, pointing to the horizon where the werewolves were standing.

"Deryck, they are on the move!"

"Is your phone still on? Can Justin still hear us?"

Tim nodded, "yes."

"Right, listen, Justin, I'm going to drag you to the window on the side of the pub... Let me know when you are at the window, looking at the sides of the cab. You should be about a foot from the window... We'll have to act quick. Sarah will have to have her door unlocked for us to get in... Sarah, you go through the window to the pub first, so there is space in the cab for Tim and me... let's do this!"

As Deryck finished speaking, he started to turn into the pub carpark. They slowly crawled to the side of the pub. This had taken longer than they had hoped, it was now four O'clock, and the sun had now deserted them, leaving them to the mercy of the full moon. They could hear the howling from the beasts, which was getting louder as they got closer. The second night would be a long night for those stuck at the Tan Hill Inn, and some of them may not make it out alive.

Chapter Ten

Deryck drove past the window and had to turn suddenly to miss his garage in front of him. Justin rapidly slammed on the brakes as they got level with the window. He shouted "stop" down the phone to Deryck.

"Well done, turn your lights on full beam, Justin," shouted Deryck, "Sarah, make sure that the door is unlocked for Tim and me, or we are fucked!"

Justin looked towards the pub window as he turned the lights on. They were greeted by the face of Simon, who was staring back at him through the window, with his thumbs up.

"You ready, Sarah? ... Unlock your door!" said Justin, as he wound down his window and turned to Simon, "the gap is two-feet wide... it is going to be risky. Sarah, come on. Be careful as you climb through the windows."

Simon opened the sash window to let them in. He had three others with him to help, Paul from the stag party, Glenn, and George from the band. They were all ready to collect the rescue party and the food.

"Hello there, do you have a booking?" laughed Simon, "come on, Sarah, ladies first!"

Sarah climbed over Justin towards the window. Whilst Sarah stretched through the windows to Simon, Justin held her waist and then her legs as Simon and Paul pulled her to the safety of the pub.

"You ok, Sarah?" asked Justin, "Hey, is there something we can stretch from window to window, so we can send this food over. This gap is a bit of a stretch. We could be at risk now."

As Justin asked, Simon sent through a board that had just reached the cab. Justin started to send boxes over to Simon, which he passed to the others.

"Fuck, did you hear that? They are getting closer," whispered Justin.

"Where are the other two?" asked Simon.

Justin pointed over to Deryck and Tim, still sitting in the stationary tractor.

Deryck took a deep breath and then climbed down from the tractor and ran towards the lorry. Tim quickly followed him, even though he was still in pain from his fall, earlier. The vodka that Tim had been drinking had taken the edge of his pain. However, he was drunk, and staggered to the lorry. Although the werewolves could not be seen, their howls were scarily deafening. As Deryck opened the passenger's door, Justin greeted him.

"Deryck, quick get in!"

Deryck climbed up into the relative safety of the cab. "We are too late. They are on top of us, now!" came the panicked voice of Deryck as he made way for Tim. Just as Tim, still holding the bottle of vodka, was about to climb into the cab. He was suddenly dragged back into the snow by the female werewolf. The male beast watched his mate, as he stood on top of the cab. Tim called out for help as he laid in the snow, the female beast looking over him. Tim attempted to crawl towards the lorry, but the werewolf grabbed his leg and then let go, toying with the injured man. The werewolf seized Tim's leg for a second time, pulling him back. As Tim looked up at Deryck, he winked at him, and then he took a swipe at the beast with his right fist, whilst he still held the bottle. The rest of the vodka poured down Tim's arm.

"Oh, what a waste!" Tim said to himself.

The werewolf was quicker than Tim and ripped through his throat and again at his chest, opening it up. Deryck called out to Tim, but he quickly closed the door, locking it, knowing there was nothing he could do. Concerned about his friend, Paul stretched out of the window and called for him, making him vulnerable.

"Tim, Tim, are you ok? ... Tim, Tim!" cried, Paul.

A fatal move, Paul's calling had attracted the werewolf on top of the cab. The creature grabbed at Paul and dragged him out into the chilly night. The werewolf had Paul dangling in front of him by the throat. The beast then held Paul by his head and glared into his victim's eyes. Paul closed his eyes as the werewolf bit through his throat, separating his head from its torso. His body fell to the floor, turning the snow from white to a deep dark red, as the blood left the corpse in the dusk of the night. The werewolf then threw Paul's head through the window, which landed onto one of the upper steps, out of sight. Watching everything, Simon, and George both vomited on the stairs.

As Justin looked down at his friend's decapitated body, he now found himself and Deryck, trapped in the lorry.

"Shit, close the windows!" shouted Simon as he pulled in the board and closed his window. Justin quickly closed his window as well. He and Deryck were now trapped inside the cab as the beasts stalked them outside. Deryck promptly closed the curtains inside the cab, hoping that the werewolves outside were unaware of the potential victims inside.

"Fuck. Tim and Paul, both gone!" cried Justin, "Tim's getting married next Saturday... to my little sister... how am I going to explain this to her... they were so in love... they have been together since school."

Justin started to panic, "What if I don't get home to tell my sister? I don't want to die here."

"Calm down, Justin. You can't lose it now... I'm so sorry, Justin, this should never have happened," explained Deryck, tearful and nervous about what had happened and what was to come. Now, Deryck is struggling with this and is on the verge of breaking.

"Look, Deryck, you need to hold it together!" stated Justin as he wiped his tears away. "You have people in your pub who need you to be strong... your wife, your team, and your customers need you to bring them out of this... we cannot mourn the dead until we are safe."

"I guess you are right, Justin, thank you."

"At least Sarah is safe. That's down to you, Deryck!" explained Justin.

"I guess so. Thanks, Justin. You're a good man."

"Even though my sister's fiancé is dead," snapped Justin, "sorry, I didn't mean that!"

"That's ok, Justin. You are right what you say."

A couple of hours had passed while the two were chatting, oblivious of what the werewolves were doing outside. Justin opened his side curtain, to see if Simon was still at the window. He could see that no one was there, and he felt despair as he turned to Deryck.

"They have gone. We are alone!" Justin said as the two looked at the empty window.

But then, suddenly, Glenn appeared at the window, and the relief of knowing they were not alone flowed through them.

"We need a plan for tomorrow to get everyone out of here... What about that all-terrain vehicle out there? Does it work?" said Justin as he looked and smiled at Glenn.

"It hasn't worked since we've been here. the trailer is connected to a generator, which we use to cook food for outdoor events," replied Deryck.

"Ok. Mind you, we have enough vehicles here. We have the bands coach to escape in. we should be ok," said Justin, "right, we need to move this lorry closer to that window!"

With the engine still running, Justin peaked through the curtains to see if the werewolves were still out there. He turned to Deryck.

"They have gone, and so have the bodies of Paul and Tim! ... we need to act fast!"

"Look, over there. They have dragged your friend's bodies over there, near those cars."

Justin signalled to Glenn to open the window. He then partly opened the curtains, put the lorry in reverse, and moved the vehicle backwards, turning the steering wheel towards the pub. He then moved forward, getting closer to the window. There was a crunch, the wing mirrors on the driver's side were destroyed, but the lorry was now less than a foot from the window. Justin stopped, pulled on the brakes, and closed the curtains again. After a few seconds, Justin and Deryck peaked through to see if they could see anything. There seemed to be nothing out there, but the two were leaving nothing to chance. Justin opened his side curtain and his window, then Glenn greeted him. Justin turned off the engine and put the keys in his pocket. He started to pass the rest of the boxes to Glenn.

"Where are the others?"

"Downstairs, Simon asked me to keep a lookout on you guys!" whispered Glenn.

"Shush, what's that noise?" whispered Deryck, "they are back... Quick Justin, get in the fucking pub!"

"But the food?"

"Fucking move!" as Deryck pushed Justin towards the window, "Glenn, pull him in."

Glenn took the box that Justin was holding, dropped it on the floor, and then grabbed Justin's arms, pulling him through the window. The two fell onto the floor, Justin on top of Glenn.

"You two look cosy down there. Would you like a room?" Deryck said from above the pair lying on the floor as he closed the window and then helped them to their feet.

"Let's get these boxes down to the kitchen. We can grab the rest tomorrow," said Deryck.

Suddenly, the three noticed that Tony was standing at the foot of the stairs.

"Hello, boss."

Sarah was with him, and she ran up the stairs and flung her arms around Deryck.

"Thank you so much for coming for me, thank you!" she cried in floods of tears.

"That's ok, sweetheart. I wasn't going to leave you out there on your own... sorry we had to leave you overnight in that cab," replied Deryck.

"Don't forget, we lost two in this rescue mission!" snapped Justin as he brushed past them with a box and headed to the bar.

"Sorry!" wept Sarah as Deryck squeezed her hand for comfort.

"Tony, where is everyone else? Where is Carol?"

"Everyone is in the restaurant. Simon and Sam are looking after them," explained Tony, "Clair is helping me in the kitchen."

"Have all the doors and windows been barricaded... why haven't you done the front door?" asked Deryck, "where's Carol?"

"We were not sure if you needed to come through there," answered Tony, "Carol is there."

As Tony pointed to an empty reception, Carol passed them at the foot of the stairs. She was oblivious of everyone, including her husband. She headed for the front door, unbolting, and unlocking it like a madwoman.

"Carol, sweetheart, you ok... Carol, wait, stop, what are you doing?... don't go out there," shouted Deryck as he ran towards his wife. She opened the door and walked out into the wintry night. The others shouted to her, "STOP!"

Deryck stood at the door, calling for his wife to come back to him

"Don't go out there. Please, sweetheart, don't go out there. Come back to me, now?"

She ignored him and continued to walk outside. The door to the bar suddenly opened, with Jon and Gary standing there. The others had gathered behind them, to see what was happening.

"What's going on?" asked Jon, "close the fucking door!"

"Shut the fuck up!" shouted Tony, pointing at the two who had joined them.

"Shush, keep quiet, you lot!" whispered Glenn.

Deryck looked outside to where his wife stood, calling for her to return. She was suddenly confronted by one of the werewolves. The second jumped down from the top of the vehicles parked out front.

Suddenly, Carol was now aware of where she was, and called for her husband. She called his name for the second time, "Deryck, help me!"

"Wait, Carol. I'm coming for you," Deryck shouted back to his wife.

The werewolves turned and looked straight at Deryck. They moved towards him, leaving Carol frozen to her spot. Just as he was about to run to his wife's aid, he was grabbed and pulled back into the pub by Glenn and Jon as Gary closed the door behind them. They heard Carol's scream and then silence.

"Let me go... Carol, Carol... fucking let me go!" Deryck sobbed, "wait, Carol, I'm coming... fucking get off me... let me go... Carol!"

As Gary locked the door, the pair held on to Deryck, "we can't risk them getting in here!" snapped Gary.

"Leave him alone... get off him!" Tony took over and led his friend to the bar, "come on, Deryck."

"Tony, let me go to her. Let me bring her back."

"She's gone, Deryck, she's gone!" Tony comforted his friend as he took him to a table near the bar. He then went to the bar and returned with a bottle, a glass, and the ice bucket. Tony poured Deryck a large glass of his favourite whiskey and then added a couple of ice cubes.

"Drink this, Deryck. It will help," said Tony as he poured himself a glass, and started to cry.

The three band members, Jon, Gary, and Glenn proceeded to take a couple of tables through to barricade the front door. Neville and Tom joined, two more of the stags, joined them, carrying another table. Tony asked Sam and Simon to go through to the kitchen to help Clare.

"You guys better go and tell Clare what has happened."

Simon held Sam, who was in tears, as they walked through to the kitchen.

He then returned his attention to his boss, holding him, "I'm so sorry, Deryck, she was a lovely woman!"

Chapter Eleven

All of the doors had been barricaded, and hopefully nothing was getting in. Simon had fitted the old router, but they only had a weak signal available. There was an eerie silence amongst everyone in the bar. The stags were consoling each other after the loss of their friends. Justin was also being comforted by his new friend, Lisa. Some were shaking with fear, scared of what was to come. Lisa's friends held each other, petrified. There were a few screams as the door to the restaurant was suddenly flung open. Brad and Lucy, who had gone to their room, rushed in.

Brad shouted, "there's a vehicle coming down the road with orange flashing lights. It's near that lorry's trailer."

"Uncle Ruby," said Alex.

"No, they are definitely orange, bro!" answered Brad

"No, it's my Uncle Ruby's gritter lorry. Uncle Paul and his partner, Detective Longland, must have got through," replied Alex as he pulled his phone from his trousers, and rang his uncle.

"Uncle Paul, can you hear me, Uncle Paul? I've lost them. Crap signal!"

The signal was too weak outside, and the call was disrupted, leaving the three on the road clueless of the situation ahead of them.

"Alex, Alex, can you hear me?" came a reply from Uncle Paul in the lorry.

"I should think he can hear you without that phone," shouted Ruby, "right down my fucking ear!"

"Sorry!" replied Paul, "lost the signal," as he threw his phone onto the dashboard.

Ruby continued driving, "Tell me, brother, why are we driving out here tonight?"

"I thought you were supposed to be working on this route tonight, anyway, Ruby?"

"I was, but not out here tonight," grunted Ruby, "I swapped with Dave so I could help you."

"It's not for me. It's for our sister's boy!"

"Yes, ok, but why?" answered Ruby.

"I got a message from Alex, earlier today. He said that he thinks there may be some trouble at the Tan Hill Inn... some madman or something."

"Hang on, you two. What's that lorry doing there?" interrupted Nathan, "the back doors are open!"

"What the fuck! Looks like it's been hijacked," said Ruby as he drove alongside the abandoned trailer. He stopped his vehicle and turned to Paul and Nathan.

"What the fuck is going on?"

Now, Paul and Ruby Coman were the younger brothers of Alex's mum, Victoria. When Ruby was born, he was red faced, and his sister, who was five at the time, called him Ruby. The name had stuck ever since, which caused problems at school. Due to this, Ruby was a tough lad and got into many fights. When he was old enough, Ruby joined the army, which, most definitely kept him out of prison. Ruby left the army when he was thirty, he had been driving lorries ever since. Paul was two years younger than his brother and joined the North Yorkshire police when he was eighteen. Paul and Nathan

Longland went through training together and had been friends ever since. They supported each other through the deaths of their wives, through cancer. Now the two worked together in CID, both as detective sergeants.

As Paul and Nathan sat looking out of the window, Ruby turned off the engine. The three climbed down from the warmth of their cab to look around the scene. Ruby went to the back of the trailer, shining his torch to see inside. Nathan and Paul headed to the front, where the cab should be. They shone their torches, in the hope to find clues.

"Look at the size of these footprints," whispered Nathan, "what the hell size of dog made them? They are bigger than a Great Dane."

"It looks like two of them, and they are walking on their hind legs... fucking hell, look at that pile of snow, it's red."

The pair of them pointed their torches towards the pile of snow where Max was buried. Some of the snow had been blown away, revealing Max's hair. Ruby joined his brother and Nathan at the front of the trailer with a cold pie in his hand.

"Poor bastard, what happened to him?"

"No idea, maybe he got hit by the lorry, and the driver fled in the cab?" answered Paul.

"Oh, I guess the owners of these footprints did the decent thing and buried the body?" replied Ruby sarcastically, "Great detective work! ... Did you miss the two sets of tyres in the snow? It looks like one vehicle was towing the other. Maybe a tractor towing the lorries cab?"

The pair ignore his comment, looking back at Max's temporary grave and then at Ruby. Paul then said to Nathan exactly what Ruby had just mentioned.

"I think you are right there, partner," replied Nathan.

"Whatever!" said Ruby as he walked away.

"Hang on, where did you get that pie?" asked Nathan

"Off the back of a lorry, you going to arrest me?"

"Let's have a look!" said Nathan as the three walked to the back of the trailer to take a look.

"This food was going to the Tan Hill Inn. Looks like whoever was here has taken some food with them... and in a hurry," stated Paul.

"Lying bastards!" said Nathan.

"What?"

"You remember, when we took the girls to the Tan Hill for a meal, all them years ago... those at the pub, told us that they made their own pies!" answered Nathan as he bit into a pie he had picked up, "hang on, they're still frozen in the middle... how the hell can you eat that?"

The pie was thrown to the floor, and Ruby picked it up.

"You weird git, how is he your brother Paul?"

"Not sure, he'll eat anything... he often shares his food with Blake."

"Mustn't waste food!" stated Ruby, "Blake will eat that."

The three looked up at Ruby's window. Blake, now sitting in the driver's seat, was looking back at them, panting, and cleaning himself. He was Ruby's dog, which was crossed between a Spaniel and a Rottweiler. He was a funny mix, but he looked more like a black Labrador. Blake had been asleep on the back seat for the entire journey.

"Let's go!" said Paul.

The three climbed back into the gritter lorry. Ruby handed the frozen pie to his dog. Blake took the pie and then returned to the back seat. He left his treat at one end of his blanket and returned to the other end, where he was sleeping.

"Looks like Blake is fussier about his food than you are," chuckled Paul, followed by a laugh from Nathan.

"Ha-ha!" replied Ruby as he started the engine and pulled away in the direction of the pub.

As they got closer to the pub, still laughing, and joking about Ruby's appetite, they saw the lorry cab and the tractor it was still tied to, in the carpark.

"Well, that's what happened to the cab," said Ruby.

"Yes. It looks like we were correct, Paul," said Nathan.

"Yes, Nathan. It does."

"What? ... Wait, you two," interrupted Ruby, "over there in the pub carpark... what the fuck are they?" as he pointed in the direction of the pub. The two werewolves stood about eight feet tall on their hind legs, howling at the moon. They were standing near the all-terrain vehicle, away from the lorries.

"Shit, those things must have been what Alex was on about," said Ruby as he stopped his lorry, "what are we going to do?"

"You will do nothing but wait in your lorry," Paul stated to his brother, "we're the police, not you!"

As police detectives in the Criminal Investigation Department, they were lawfully allowed service issue pistols. Unlawfully, they had managed to sign a couple out for the weekend with the help of their friend, the sergeant who dealt with such paperwork.

"What are you going to do with those pea-shooters?" laughed Ruby. He stretched over to his back seat and introduced his baby to the other two, his Beretta Silver Pigeon shotgun.

"There you go, boys, that'll take em down!"

"What the fuck... what the hell are you doing with that in your cab? That's supposed to be locked up at home, not in your lorry!" said Paul.

"I always bring it with me while clearing the roads around here. It makes me and Blake feel safe, doesn't it, boy."

"Well, he can't take it home now, and it will come in handy, Paul."

"Shut up. Whose side are you on, Nathan?"

"Well, technically, we shouldn't have these guns either," said Nathan.

"Oh yeh, why is that?" asked Ruby.

"You don't need to know!" Paul snapped as he confiscated Ruby's shotgun.

"Hey!"

"I'll look after that; you look after this," as he hands his pistol to his brother. "Right, now that feels a lot better. Where's your ammo, bro?"

Ruby reluctantly pointed to a case on the back seat, as he sat there, not happy with his brother. Paul just smiled at him and retrieved a supply of ammo from the case.

"Bloody hell, are you expecting a war? there's enough ammo in here to take out an army."

"Right, now you two have sorted yourselves out. We need to get this thing in that car park," said Nathan, "let's go!"

Ruby smiled back at his brother as he started his lorry, and moved forward cautiously, as the other two kept an eye on the car park, which was now empty.

The werewolves had disappeared from sight. Perhaps, being scared off by the sight of the lorry?

"Where have those creatures gone?" asked Nathan, "I can't see a damn thing!"

"Look there, that bloke looks dead!" said Paul as he pointed at Tim's corpse, "shit, there are two bodies there."

Ruby turned into the carpark. He pointed towards Max's lorry, "Is that woman there dead?"

He had spotted what looked like Carol's body. She was lying seemingly lifeless, face down in the snow underneath Max's lorry.

"Pull up next to that lorry... I still can't see those creatures," declared Nathan.

"Look, on top of the cab," Ruby softly replied, "there's one up there."

"Sound your horn, Ruby. Try and scare it off,"

With that, Ruby pushed on his horn which startled the werewolf. The beast climbed up the pub and scrambled over the roof, out of sight. Still pressing on his horn, Ruby could see the pub curtains move, and faces looking out.

"Hang on, that woman under there just moved... she's still alive!" said Nathan as he signalled to her to stay still, "can anyone see the other one?"

"No... where the fuck are they?"

"There's one of them... over there with what looks like... another victim," replied Paul, "Ruby, look up at that window... it's Alex."

"The other one has joined it... look!" said Nathan, pointing over at the werewolves.

The two werewolves startled by the lorry, stood over the bodies of Paul and Tim, which had been dragged over to Simon's land rover, on the other side of the car park.

The three looked back up at the window, partially obscured by Max's cab, where they could just see Alex, standing with Brad and Justin. Alex waved his phone at his uncle and then rang Ruby's phone. Ruby's phone started to ring, and he took it from his pocket to answer his nephew's call.

"Alex, how are you guys doing in there?"

"Didn't Uncle Paul get my last message?" asked Alex, "I told you not to come... it's too dangerous... seven people have been killed so far."

"Calm down, boy... we're here now," explained Ruby, "we've got guns with us."

"I'm sorry I dragged you guys into this shit!" said Alex, "how come you are alone, any more police coming?"

"No... them two didn't report this... they wanted to crack the case on their own... Supercop's, not," answered Ruby.

"Typical of them two... the stupidest coppers in Yorkshire!"

"You're right there, Alex. I would have said stupidest cops in the country," laughed Ruby.

"Shush... give me that phone!" snapped Paul, "Alex, how's everything in there... how can we get in?"

"Climb through the cab window, then through this window onto the stairs."

"We need to get a lady in, along with Ruby and Blake," said Paul, "while we dispatch these beasts!"

"Hang on, did you say lady?"

"Yes, she's hiding under the cab. She must be freezing under there!"

"My God. That must be the landlady, Carol... is she ok?"

"She looks cold... but seems unhurt," explained Paul, "other than that, she looks ok."

"You all need to get in here," stated Alex, "Uncle Paul... don't go out there!"

"Look, boy, we'll be ok... we'll kill these things, and we can all go home," replied Paul, "get ready to get the woman and your Uncle Ruby in there with you... Ok, let's do this!"

"You lot be careful out there!... we'll be ready for you." Alex then finished the call.

Paul turned to the other two, looking hyped up.

"Right, you two. We need to get everyone in that lorry and to the safety of the pub. Alex will help you through the window," explained Paul, "Ruby, hold on to Blake... make sure that woman is ok, and get her to safety... me and Nathan will cover you."

"Nathan and I!" stated Nathan.

"What?"

"It is Nathan and me. Not me and Nathan."

Ruby put his hand to his mouth and sniggered.

"Shut the fuck up! Ruby, give my pistol to Nathan."

The other two laughed uncontrollably as Ruby handed over his brother's firearm to Nathan.

"Right, when you two are ready... let's do this."

Nathan opened his door and climbed down from the lorry, followed by his colleague. Both stood between the two lorries, which functioned as great cover from the two werewolves, especially with the door open. Paul knelt down to check on Carol, whilst Nathan opened the door of Max's cab.

"Hello madam, are you ok? Take my hand... we'll get you back to safety."

Carol looked at him and shook her head. She looked scared, and frozen as she put her hands over her head. Suddenly, her face was licked by a warm tongue, as she was comforted by the gentle giant that was Blake. He seemed to have relaxed her, and she took Paul's hand. As Carol crawled from under the lorry, and stood up, she grabbed Paul and gave him a hug. Ruby was holding the lead as Carol bent down to thank her new four-legged friend. She gave him a biscuit which she had in her pocket, and Blake felt her pain and was aware of the cause. After taking the biscuit, he slipped his lead and ran, barking toward the two culprits.

"Blake, Blake, get back here... Blake!" shouted Ruby, scared for his dog's safety.

Blake stood there growling at the two werewolves, and they suddenly turned and snarled at Blake. He turned and ran back to the safety of his owner.

"Quick, get them in there, Ruby, do your fucking job!"

Ruby lifted Blake into the cab, followed by Carol, and then he climbed in himself. He was greeted by the familiar face of his nephew through the window of the pub. Alex opened the window, and he was pushed to the floor as he was greeted by Blake's tongue. Justin and Brad helped Carol through the window and wrapped her in a warm blanket as she suddenly burst into tears.

"Someone will be glad to see you, woman... are you ok?"

"I'm so sorry about what happened to your brother, Brad!" said Carol as she hugged him.

Outside, the two werewolves were now aware of their new dinner guests. They had started to prowl towards the lorries.

"Quick, you two, get up here now!" shouted Ruby

"You get in there, Ruby. We'll cover you."

"For fuck sake, get in here... they know you are there!" Ruby shouted frustratedly, "one of them has gone... quick, get in here!"

"We'll be ok... we've got this," replied Paul as he closed the door to the lorry. He looked at his partner and nodded. Nathan nodded back at him. The two policemen started shooting at the werewolf in front of them. They could only see one, who they hit in the left arm twice.

Paul stopped to reload the shotgun, "Where has the other one gone?"

Nathan shot both pistols at the werewolf, and the bullets missed her as he emptied both guns. There was a sudden growl from above them, and as they looked up, the males warm drool dripped onto their faces. The second werewolf looked down at them, straddled between the two lorries. He grabbed down at the detective's heads and twisted them clean off. Their lifeless bodies fell to the floor as the werewolf tossed their heads away. Then the night returned to silence as the two werewolves started to feast on the detectives. Ruby sat in shock at what he had just seen, and he drew the curtain shut, to block out the horrific view. With a tear rolling down Ruby's face, Blake re-joined his owner, and laid his head in his owner's lap.

Alex called to his uncle, "where is Uncle Paul?"

Ruby, with a flood of tears, turned to his nephew and shook his head. Alex slumped to his feet, knowing it was his fault that his uncle and Nathan were dead.

"Uncle Ruby, get in here, please."

"Give me a minute, Alex," replied Ruby as he stroked Blake, and cried for his brother.

Chapter Twelve

Carol was now back in the relative safety of her own home and back in the land of the living. Alex sat on the stairs, near his uncle, both in tears. Justin and Brad, holding Carol's hand, took her downstairs to the restaurant, to her grieving husband.

"Carol, how the hell did you survive that? We were sure you were dead."

"When you dragged Deryck back into the pub, I just ran. That split second gave me enough time to get to the lorry and hide."

As they walked into the restaurant, everyone looked up in amazement. Putting his index finger to his mouth, Justin signalled so that everyone would keep quiet as Brad walked Carol over to Deryck. Deryck was still seated, a solitary man on a lone table, with a solitary bottle of whiskey to comfort him. He studied the marks on the surface of the table.

"Deryck, we have found someone you might be interested in," said Brad as Simon came over and joined them, and everyone cheered as Deryck looked up at his wife. Simon beckoned everyone to be quiet.

"Oh, hello Carol... I think we need to refurbish these tables," answered the drunken host, "how was the weather outside?"

Now, Deryck seemed to be in the same state that his wife was in before she ventured outside, but a lot calmer. Carol sat down in front of her husband and took his hands.

"Oh sweetheart, I am so sorry for being a cow this weekend. I'm sorry to everyone for losing the plot and being such a bitch," wept Carol, "I'm also sorry for leaving the back door to the office open."

"What?" snapped Simon.

"I was angry with everyone... I was angry with you, Deryck!"

"So, you left a door open for those things to get in here?" complained Brad, "fuck sake, it gets better and better!"

"Watch your tongue, boy... don't speak to my wife like that," snapped Deryck, "I'll put you on your arse!"

"I'm sorry, Brad, I wasn't...."

Simon interrupted, "It's too late for fighting and blaming each other... we need to get that door closed."

"My husband is still out there on the stairs," replied Amber. "His uncles are out there!"

"Those two poor men and that poor man stuck in that lorry!" muttered Carol.

"What are you on about woman?" barked Deryck.

"Alex's uncles, Paul and Ruby, along with a friend, came to help," explained Amber, "Uncle Paul and his colleague Nathan are police detectives. Uncle Ruby brought them here in his gritter lorry."

"The two men with guns are dead. That nice man and his dog are still in the lorry," Carol repeated as she started to cry.

"What, my husband's uncle is dead? Shit, my poor Alex."

Amber went to join her husband on the stairs, to comfort him.

Just at that moment, Tony walked through from the kitchen, and saw Carol.

"Carol, you're alive... give me a hug."

"Tony, I need your help. We need to close the back door of the office... it's been left open," said Simon.

"What idiot did that?" replied Tony.

"I'll just go through to the kitchen and see the girls," said Carol sheepishly as she headed to the kitchen.

"Come on, Tony, let's do this," said Simon, "Brad, keep everyone here.

The two staff members headed for the bar's exit, closing the door behind them. Tony and Simon were now in the foyer with Alex and Amber, sitting by the window. They were joined by Justin, who went up the stairs to let Alex and Amber know what was happening. Simon made sure that the bar door was shut, whilst Tony moved to the office door. Tony put his ear to the door to see if he could hear anything. He heard something on the other side and signalled to the others.

"I can hear them on the other side of the door."

Simon moved towards Tony, and Alex signalled to his uncle to keep quiet. Tony was still at the door when it suddenly crashed down on top of him, trapping him to the floor. He was now hidden from the male werewolf, standing on top of the door. Simon was in a vulnerable position, just metres from the werewolf on the other side of the reception desk. Simon looked up at Alex, Amber and Justin and whispered to them to hide. Alex helped his wife through the window into the cab. He then let Justin crawl through the window, back into the lorry where he had been earlier when his friends were killed. Simon then looked back at the werewolf and then down at his friend, Tony. The werewolf was looking straight at Simon.

Simon shouted out. "Brad, it's too late... barricade that door... they are in...."

Simon's warning was cut short as the werewolf pounced on him, pushing Simon to the floor. The werewolf savagely tore at Simon's chest with her claws, and then ripped his throat out with her teeth. The beast stood above Simon, dripping his blood onto him as life quickly deserted him. Alex promptly escaped through the window, into the unexpected safety of Max's lorry. He was greeted by a hug from his wife. He then turned and tried to reach the sash window to close it, but he was unsuccessful. Ruby went to turn the keys so he could close the cab window.

"Where are the keys?"

Justin tried his pocket, "shit, I think I must have left them inside?"

"Simon is dead!" whispered Alex.

The sash window was still open, and no key to close the cab window. The group only had a curtain to protect them from the beast. Ruby held Blake to keep him quiet, as he had barked when the three had climbed through and joined them. They now sat in total silence, but they could hear the werewolf breathing on the stairs.

Meanwhile, Brad cautiously opened the restaurant door and took a peek. He was confronted with the body of Simon, and then he noticed Tony, still lying under the door, staring back at him. Tony signalled to him to go back and secure the door. Brad Looked up at the beast's feet on the stairs and then back at Tony, just as the other werewolf came from the office and stepped on the door. The female standing on the door had been injured, shot by the two policemen dead outside. Brad could see her blood dripping just millimetres from Tony's head. The old chef would need a miracle to get out of this predicament. Not been seen yet, Brad reluctantly retreated and closed the door in front of him. He then signalled to the others to bring tables over to barricade the door and then walked over to Deryck to tell him the sad news of Simon.

"Oh fuck, poor lad... what are we going to do... we are not going to get through this night," cried Deryck.

Deryck stood and headed towards the kitchen to tell his girls the sad news. Over the last twenty-four hours, Deryck had aged so much that he entered the kitchen a drunk and broken man.

"Carol, girls... I've got some sad news... Simon and Tony... Simons is dead, and tony is trapped with those beasts."

Carol fell to the floor in hysterics as Clare and Sam held each other, crying. Simon had been an integral part of Carol and Deryck's team for four years. He was loved by all his colleagues, and he was excellent with the customers. Carol was especially fond of Simon, as if he were her own. She had told Deryck before, that Simon's presence had helped with the loss of their late son.

Despite of what was happening just metres away, in the foyer, those in the kitchen started to prepare a feast for later. It may be a celebration feast after the beasts had been killed, or it may never be tasted by the guests. The kitchen now had plenty of food to use, which had been delivered from Max's lorry. Carol had no intention of doing anything with this food after this weekend. They may perish before the food did, and they could not think that far ahead. The opinion was that it was getting late, and people were hungry. Also, the cooking helped with the kitchen's grief after Simon's death.

••••◄❰❱►••••

Chapter Thirteen

Meanwhile, in Max's cab were three very scared people, who sat in complete darkness. Alex and Amber held each other, as they sat on the back seat with Justin. Ruby sat in his seat with Blake lying on his lap, as he wept for his brother. The silence was deafening, you could hear a pin drop, or at least the sound of a werewolf breathing on the other side of the lorry's curtains. The werewolf was close and could smell them as he pushed on the curtain through the open windows.

Everyone in the cab tensed up, and the silence was broken by a loud fart. The three youngsters looked at Ruby as they tried to stop themselves from laughing. The curtain was pulled aside, and the beast looked into the dark cab, and sniffed the air. He had not found them yet, and the smell was unpleasant.

Suddenly, a loud noise from outside distracted the werewolves. The sound of a customised car horn disturbed the night as an unexpected vehicle sped into the carpark, breaking precipitously because these guys, at least the driver, did not care about anyone else. These four men in their early thirties had travelled up from London and wanted to have a lot of fun. They were rich, posh, and arrogant... well, at least the driver was. This was just the miracle that Tony was hoping for.

Alex peaked through the curtain of the lorry cab, "who the fuck are these guys?"

At the same time, Brad was looking through one of the windows, thinking the same thing, as the four got out of their vehicle and headed for the front door. He looked at Lucy.

"Who the hell are these guys?"

"Don't know... but it might help get them monsters out of the building?"

Alex climbed over to the front seat and moved the curtain in front of him. They watched, as the car turned into the carpark.

"Who are these guys?" whispered Justin as he held his nose.

"Not sure, but their noise has saved us from that werewolf."

"Yes, and the noise from your uncle's arse let him know where we were," said Amber as the three started to laugh. "It stunk, what the hell have you been eating?"

"Shut up, you three. At least the smell put that thing off us."

The driver turned the door handle of the pub, only to find that the door was locked and bolted. He rang the doorbell and knocked on the door.

"Hello, anyone there? Why is your door locked?" shouted the driver.

"What the hell is going on? There are a lot of vehicles in the carpark. All of the curtains are closed," said one of the others.

Two of them start shouting, kicking, and banging on the door.

"Hello, is there anyone about? Let us in!" said the driver. The driver returned to his Range Rover and started pressing the horn again.

The fourth guy, who up until now had been quiet, noticed Brad at the window and approached him.

"Can you let us in?" he asked.

One of the others approached, "let us in, you bastard!"

Unable to hear what they were saying, Brad smashed one of the window panels.

"You need to get back in your vehicle and get away from here as quick as possible," warned Brad.

"Fuck you, you prick... open the fucking door... do you know who we are?" replied the second one, who was told to shut up by the first.

"No, it's nine o'clock. I'm cold and hungry. Open the fucking door, you fucking pricks." shouted the second man as he returned to banging on the front door.

Chloe joined Brad at the window, "Brad, let me, this one is my brother... David, what are you doing here?"

"Hiya Chloe, I said we might join you this weekend... what's going on?"

"You need to go home... get away from here... people are dead. Did you not see the bodies?" replied Chloe.

"What are you going on about?"

"There's a couple of beasts out there. They are dangerous."

"I know, but you're not normally bothered by Boris and Edward," laughed David.

"What? I am being serious, David. This is no joke... are you on drugs?"

"Just a bit of blow, sis."

"Ahh, Chloe, let me in... then you can come upstairs and get naked with me," interrupted Edward, the one had spoken to Brad, with David.

"Fuck off, Edward. Hell will freeze over first."

"You wait... I'll get you high and then I'll get you into my bed," replied Edward, with which David threw a punch at his mate.

"Don't talk to my sister like that, you bastard."

Being a lot bigger than David, Edward returned a punch, striking David to the ground, knocking him unconscious.

"You bastard... David, David, are you ok," Chloe cried as her friends led her away from the window, "no, we need to get David in here... I don't care if those wankers die... but not my brother."

"Chloe, we can't let him in at the moment. Those werewolves could get in," said Gina.

"What the hell are they doing here? They are always about when there is trouble. Trouble and them four come hand in hand," replied Charlotte.

Brad closed the curtains again, keeping a close eye on the four men. The fourth group member, Michael, had decided to walk around the building. He wanted to find another way into the pub. Boris, irritating as he is, was still filling the night air with his horn, which would be the groups downfall. Michael approached the two lorries as he noticed Ruby's face looking through the curtains.

"Won't they let you in as well?" laughed Michael

"You need to get out of here... you're not safe."

"What?... fuck you, you prick." Michael stuck his two fingers up aggressively and returned to his friends, hurling abuse at those in the pub.

David had woken up, still shaken with blood oozing from his nose. he was on his own outside as his friends had turned against him, as usual. He picked himself up off the ground and brushed himself down.

Brad called to him, "hey buddy, get yourself to the side of the building. There are people in the lorry there… tell them that Brad sent you."

David nodded back at Brad as he held his bloody nose, he started to make his way to the lorries at the side of the pub.

"Where are you going, you wimp?" shouted Edward.

"Just going to find a way in," replied a sheepish David.

"Oh, fuck off then, you prick… I'm going to have your sister later."

"We all are!" shouted Boris.

David ignored them as he disappeared out of sight, and the three returned to creating the noise that they were making earlier.

Meanwhile, back in the foyer of the pub, with Tony still stuck under the door. The noise outside had drawn the attention of the two werewolves. Standing on top of Tony, the female looked up at the male, standing on the stairs. She turned around and headed back into the office for the open door leading outside to their new victims. The male headed down the stairs to follow his mate, stepping again on top of Tony, who was frozen stiff, scared of moving. Tony looked up at the sash window, to be greeted by the face of Alex, just as the second werewolf disappeared into the office. Tony looked at him and shook his head. Alex nodded and climbed through the window back into the pub.

"Where are you going?" asked the other two.

"Wait here, I think they have gone back outside… because of the noise… I'm going to check on that chef and close that door that they got in through," whispered Alex.

"Be careful!" replied his wife.

Alex crept down the stairs and cowered behind the reception desk, and he peeked round to see Tony. The female werewolf had heard a noise and returned to the doorway. Alex was just able to duck back behind the desk before the werewolf was able to see him. He sat there on the floor, scared of what might happen, with his eyes closed, expecting the worse. Alex waited about five minutes before he had a look to see if the coast was clear. He peeked around just as the werewolf headed back into the office. He waited a few seconds before he looked down at Tony.

"Are you ok?" whispered Alex.

Tony nodded as he still lay under the door.

"You stay there while I go and shut that door."

Alex walked across the door laying in his way, "sorry."

"Ouch, that's ok," replied Tony from beneath the door.

Alex stopped where the door used to be. He looked into an empty room and turned to Tony, giving him a thumbs up.

"They have gone."

Alex crawled to the back door of the office and closed it. He sat up against the door, relieved, temporarily blocking it for a few seconds, just to catch his breath. Alex took a look around the office, scrutinising what he could use to secure the door. Alex started with two tall steel cabinets next to the door, laying them down on top of each other. He then stood the large desk on its end, leaning it against the door. Alex then pushed a couple of small cabinets underneath the bottom legs of the desk and tipped a large bookcase onto the lot, jamming it all between the door and the wall. He then sat down on a chair.

"Nothing is getting in there."

He then stood up and walked through to the reception, lifting the door off, a tired Tony.

"Leave me under here... I'm safe under this door. Put it back, please!" whispered Tony.

"It's ok now. They are back outside... I've barricaded the door," said Alex as he ran over to the bar.

He banged on the door, calling for Brad, "it's safe. You can open the door now."

Brad opened the door and looked out into the foyer. Alex was helping Tony over to the door, and Brad gave them a hand. There came a cheer as the three walked into the bar, but the three asked them to keep quiet.

"This is not over yet," said Alex as he headed back to the stairs.

Carol came through from the kitchen to see the commotion, and then she saw Tony.

"Tony, you are safe," she said as she ran across the room and flung her arms around him, "are you ok?"

"Yes, I'm ok. A bit tired, and my legs have gone after being under that door all that time."

"Well, come into the kitchen with me. The girls need cheering up... and we could do with a hand," asked Carol.

"Let him rest, Carol," said Deryck.

"I'm ok, Deryck. After all that, I could do with getting in my kitchen. I could do with a stiff drink as well," replied Tony as he picked up a bottle of gin and followed Carol into the kitchen.

Meanwhile, back outside, David had walked up to the driver's door of Max's lorry, when he suddenly slipped on something. Thinking it was the snow, he looked down to be greeted by the headless corpses of the two detectives. Shocked, he looked up at the faces of Ruby and his dog, Blake.

"Brad said you will let me in... I'm Chloe's brother."

Ruby turned to Justin, "Chloe?"

"One of the girls... one of Lisa's friends," replied Justin.

"Who is Lisa?" said Ruby.

Ruby looked at Justin, then at David, and again at Justin. "Justin, get yourself and Amber inside the pub... take my Blake with you."

"What are you going to do?"

"Don't worry, we'll be behind you... I need a pint."

Amber started to climb through the windows, just as her husband grabbed hold of her, and helped her. The two stood on the stairs and kissed. Justin took hold of Blake's collar and then led him through the window. Blake seemed comfortable being led by his new friend, but he still looked back at his owner for assurance.

"Don't worry, boy, I'll be with you soon."

Ruby then turned his attention to David, still outside in the chilly night. Ruby opened his door and pointed out his hand. Thinking it was there to help him up, David took his hand.

Ruby pulled it away, giving him a firm "No," he again pointed at the floor.

"Pass me those weapons," said Ruby.

"What?"

"Pick up those guns down there on the floor... pass them to me, quick."

David looked down at the two bodies, still holding their weapons. He then looked across the carpark from between the two lorries to see one of the werewolves pass his view.

"Quick, there is another one of them things out here with us," said Ruby.

David knelt down to the two detectives and grabbed at the shotgun, snap. He had to break a couple of Paul's fingers to release the gun from his grip.

135

"Hey, be careful. That's my fucking brother, you bastard."

"Sorry, I couldn't loosen it from his hand," whispered David as he passed the gun to Ruby.

He then retrieved the pistols from Nathan's death grip and passed them to Ruby. Ruby moved over to the driver's seat so that David could climb up into the cab.

"Close that door behind you," said Ruby as he climbed through the window. David watched as he disappeared into the pub. Ruby's head then reappeared back through the window.

"Pass me them guns, lad!"

David grabbed the guns, one at a time, and passed them through the window to Ruby. David was about to climb through when Ruby told him to hand him the case from the back seat first.

"For fuck sake, I want to get out of here!"

"You will... as soon as you pass me that case!"

David grabbed the case and pushed it through the window at Ruby.

"What the fuck have you got in there? It's bloody heavy."

Ruby took it from him and headed down the stairs. David climbed through the window behind him.

"Thanks for the help," said David.

"You're in, aren't you?" replied Ruby, "Close that fucking window!"

David closed the sash window and headed downstairs. Alex was now waiting for his uncle at the open door of the bar, with Amber and Blake.

"Uncle Ruby!" said Alex as they hugged each other, "I'm so sorry about Uncle Paul." The two started to cry.

"Well, this is all cosy. Are we going to let my friends in now?"

"Look, mate, we are not opening them doors for anyone. If those werewolves get in here, we're all dead," shouted Alex.

"Oi, David, let us in, you fucking prick!" came a voice from the other side of the door.

David started to remove the barricade, so he could let his so-called friends in, until he was stopped by the gentle touch of his sister.

"They are not worth the lives of everyone in this building, David!" Chloe softly stated to her brother. She then called out to David's friends in the hope of making them see sense.

"Edward, you guys are not safe out there... you need to get in your car and get away from here... now!"

"Fuck off bitch!" came the reply from David's friends.

Chloe shrugged her shoulders at her brother and walked back into the bar to be with her girls. David followed her, knowing what she had said was correct.

"I'm sorry, Chloe. I know they can be dicks, but we have been friends since school."

"Fuck off, David. They don't give a shit about you," said Charlotte.

"They always take the piss out of you, David," said Gina, smiling at him, "they don't deserve you as a friend. You are too nice."

"You are thirty, David. It's about time you grew up," said Chloe.

"That's a bit harsh, Chloe. He is your brother," replied Gina.

"Yes, I know, but he pisses me off sometimes. I do love him... but not as much as you do, Gina," laughed Chloe as Lisa and Charlotte cheered her on.

David left the girls and approached the table where Ruby was standing near one of the windows. Ruby had positioned himself at the window with the pane of glass missing. His shotgun was pushed through the empty space, aimed at but not intended for the three lads.

"Thanks for helping me out there... sorry about your brother and his friend. My sister just told me that you guys came to help," said David.

"You're ok, lad. How are you feeling?" Ruby asked, "talk to your friends through this window... try and make them see sense."

David nodded and moved to the window, banging on it to get Edward's attention. Boris and Michael were not in the ideal place as they sat in their car with the engine running and music playing loud. They could not hear the werewolves' howling with all the noise they were making. Edward noticed David at the window and approached him.

"You going to let us in, you traitor?"

"Edward, you need to get out of here... it's not safe out there," David tried to explain to his friend, "I've seen them. They are huge."

"We'll handle them... we're not wimps like you," replied Edward, who then turned his attention to Ruby.

"Who the fuck are you, you old prick... Yorkshire's answer to Rambo?"

"You should listen to your friend!" said Ruby as he passed one of the pistols through the window to Edward and then pointed to the werewolves, who had joined them, "too late!"

Edward took the pistol and turned just in time to see Michael pulled from the car by one of the werewolves.

"What the fuck!" said Edward.

The wounded female werewolf was still strong enough to pull a full-grown man from the car. She now had him pinned to the floor. Hearing his friend shout for help and never shooting a gun before, Edward fired indiscriminately at the beast. Edward wounded the werewolf in her hand, which was wrapped around Michael's throat. The werewolf pulled her hand away suddenly, spilling blood everywhere. Was it her blood?

"Yes, I got you, bitch. Mess with me, and you are fucked," shouted a jubilant Edward.

"Edward, what have you done?" David shouted.

Edward looked back at Michael, to see the true extent of the damage inflicted by his bullet. The bullet had passed straight through the hand of the werewolf and penetrated Michael's neck, tearing through his jugular vein, and smashing his neck vertebrae.

"Michael, Michael, I'm sorry. What have I done!" cried Edward as those in the pub, looked on in horror?

Michael laid there, struggling for breath, as the snow around him turned red. The werewolf looked up, straight at Edward as he wet himself with fear. She left Michael and headed towards Edward, snarling at him. Panicking, Edward started to shoot at the beast, but this time missing her until the gun clicked.

"No more bullets. I'm empty," said Edward.

"You are!" replied Ruby, looking at Edward's wet patch. David pushed the muzzle of the other pistol through the broken window and started shooting at the werewolf. The gun was suddenly knocked from David's grasp by the male werewolf, who unexpectedly appeared from the left side of the window. The gun was knocked to the feet of Edward, now with both werewolves bearing down on him. Edward quickly stooped to the floor, picked up the gun, and started firing. Nothing happened, the gun jammed, damaged by the werewolf. The two werewolves pounced on Edward, clawing at his neck and chest, splattering his blood all over the windows. Ruby took a shot, just missing the male, but the pellet hit him in the arm. The werewolves quickly moved away from the pub towards the noisy car. Boris, hiding behind his car, was now outside on his own. He shouted out to those in the pub who had left him and his friends outside.

"You fucking wankers… David, you're dead… I'll kill you myself after I fuck your sister!" Boris climbed back into his car, revved his engine, and drove forward. He was finally getting out of there.

"Hopefully, he'll make it out of here," said David.

"Who cares? He sounds like a horrible piece of work?" answered Brad, who joined the others at the window.

There was a sudden loud noise which came from outside. Brad and David looked out of the window and had noticed that Boris had crashed into the band's tour bus.

"What happened?" whispered Alex.

Ruby had kept his eyes on the carpark. He explained, "as Boris was about to leave, the werewolves jumped out in front of him. He swerved into the bus. He was driving erratically whilst still in the carpark."

They watched helplessly as Boris managed to get out of the car, and started to run along the road, slipping and sliding towards Richmond. It did not take long for the werewolves, although injured, to catch up with Boris. They played with him, taking pot-shots at Boris before striking him to the floor.

Those who watched from the pub could see the fear in his eyes. Just as the werewolves ended his life and ripped him to pieces. As Boris was killed, the moonlight faded behind clouds as if a curtain had been drawn at the end of a scene. There was a sudden change in the weather, and clouds covered the moon as it started to rain.

"What's happening?" shouted Tony as he came back from the kitchen.

"It's started to rain. The moon has been blacked out by clouds... I think we might be safe again!" answered Ruby, followed by a bark from Blake.

Outside, a final howl from the werewolves filled the pub with fear... and then there was silence.

Chapter Fourteen

T he room became silent, as everyone sat in their groups at the tables that were left.

"Mmm, hopefully, we will be safe now till the morning… like last night," said Tony as he drank some whiskey, which he needed after his ordeal.

"Maybe… However, what happens after tonight?" asked Brad, "what happens when we go our separate ways. "When we get home to our families… how are we going to cope with this, mentally?" added Lucy.

"We can all meet up here annually as an anniversary?" replied Alex.

"I'm never coming back to this godforsaken place!" said Charlotte.

"Me neither!" replied John and Ed, which was echoed by others.

Suddenly, the kitchen door opened, and Carol, Sam, and Clare came through with loads of food they had been preparing.

"Come on, everyone, tuck in," said Carol.

"Tony, give me a hand… drinks are on the house!" shouted Deryck, "Me and Carol have an announcement. This is as good a time as any to announce it… we are selling up and retiring… there's a couple coming tomorrow to look at the pub. They are getting the first offer with money off." Deryck looked at his staff, "your jobs are safe, guys!"

"Hopefully, we can celebrate with you guys," said Carol.

At this moment, Jon slipped out of the room, unseen by the others.

"What's with the silence... eat, drink, and be merry!" shouted Carol.

"Are we really going to have a fucking party with what has gone on this weekend? You people are fucking sick," snapped Gina, "there's people dead out there... who gives a fuck if you're selling up."

"I'm sorry for seeming heartless... not sure what else to do," replied Carol as her emotions improved.

"We are trying to make good of an unpleasant situation... we are all still alive. Let's celebrate that at least," said Deryck as he comforted his wife.

There was a sudden gasp from some of those in the room as the door was flung open, and in walked Jon, carrying two acoustic guitars, "come on boys, let's have a jam session."

For the next couple of hours, everyone tried to enjoy themselves, and it seemed, for a while, they had forgotten about the last two days. But, trying not to think of the horror, they still raise the odd glass to those who have gone. Max, buried in the snow, near where he parked his lorry. Mo and Jess, who had died in the pod, where they enjoyed their evening underneath the stars. The chef, James, who went for a smoke, now lying in the kitchen's courtyard with Mo and Jess. Tim, the groom, and his mate Paul, who came for his last week of freedom and now lay dead in the carpark. Detective Sergeant Longland and Detective Sergeant Coman, who came to the aid of those stricken at the Tan Hill Inn. Simon, the bartender who looked after his customers diligently and risked his life to protect his friends. Also, the three lads, however horrible, who turned up at the right time to bring the werewolves back out of the pub, saving the others.

It was one o'clock in the morning, and apart from the rain falling, outside seemed calm again. Everyone had been eating and drinking for a few hours and needed to sleep before leaving this hell hole in the morning. The staff had made the decision that everyone should keep together for the rest of the night. Carol and her team, including Tony, left the room to get bedding for everyone, leaving Deryck behind the bar. Gina and Charlotte, who offered to help to collect the bedding, joined the group. The band had noticed the group leaving the room and made comments.

"Oh, what's going on over there... that chef and all those girls... lucky him?" laughed Jon.

"You sick bugger... would you want to get naked with that Carol?" replied George as the others laughed.

"Any holes a...."

"Stop right there, young man. That's my wife, you are talking about!" laughed Deryck from the bar, "and no, you would not want to get naked with her."

The band members laughed, and the door suddenly opened with Carol standing there. They laughed again.

"What are you lot laughing about?" she asked.

"Trust me, love, you do not want to know," replied Deryck.

Tony and the girls returned to the bar with a load of bedding. It was time for everyone to try and get some sleep.

"Right guys, help yourself to some bedding... we'll all stay in here. We need try and get some sleep," shouted Deryck. "We need two people to keep watch for one-hour shifts each until the morning."

"Me, Amber and my Uncle Ruby will do the first watch," Alex replied.

"And Blake," said Amber.

"Lucy and I will relieve you in an hour," said Brad.

The offers for an hour's watch came in thick and fast until a lookout was available until the morning, and when they leave the pub. Alex, Amber and Ruby started their guard with the help of Blake. Everyone else settled down for what was left of the evening and tried to get some sleep. People huddle together in their groups, either out of fear or to keep warm. One young couple, Justin, and Lisa huddled together for their first time. Love was in the air under strange circumstances.

"Lisa, I would like to see you again, once we get away from this place."

"I would like that too, Justin."

"Cool, lets swap numbers in the morning. We better try and get some sleep," said Justin as he kissed Lisa, gently on the lips. The pair then closed their eyes to rest for a couple of hours.

Uncle Ruby and Amber were sitting at their post, chatting.

"You ok, Uncle Ruby?" asked Amber as she fussed over Blake.

"I'm ok, sweetheart. Missing my brother though... how are you and Alex?" answered Ruby as they both looked over to the window where Alex sat, keeping watch on the carpark.

"We're ok!" answered Amber as she gently squeezed Ruby's hand, "I haven't told him yet, but I'm pregnant... I was going to tell him and his parents last night, but we got stuck in the snow when Deryck found us and brought us here."

"Wow, congratulations, sweetheart... he's over there. Go and tell him now, go on."

Amber went over to her man, "Alex, I love you... how do you feel about a third joining us?"

"What... who?... that Chloe looks quite cute," Alex answered, confused. "You never told me that you were that way?"

"I'm not!" Amber slapped him and then smiled as she rubbed her belly, "this little one inside here."

"Are you serious? We're going to have a baby?" shouted Alex

The whole room cheered loudly, and then someone said, "I'm trying to sleep!" followed by "Congratulations!"

"Hang on a minute. What do you mean that Chloe is cute? Have you been eyeing up other women?" Amber asked.

"No, of course not, love. I only have eyes for you," Alex quickly replied.

"Good, and keep it that way," Amber smiled as she kissed him.

Besides the snoring and the farting from those who had eventually fallen asleep, the first hour went uneventful. Alex was joined by Brad, who had come to relieve him of his watch.

"Congratulations, bro... Go, and get some sleep, Alex!"

"I'm ok, can't sleep... I'll keep you company for a bit, Brad."

On the other side of the room, Lucy went to relieve Amber and Ruby.

"Time for beddy-buys, guys."

"Thanks, gal. Come on, Blake. Let's get some kip."

Ruby took Blake and headed over to his nephew.

"I'll stay with you for a bit Lucy," replied Amber.

Lucy gave Amber a hug, "congratulations, girl!"

"Thanks, seems unreal at the moment... with all that's going on," said Amber.

After handing his shotgun to Brad, and hugging Alex, Ruby left them and went to find somewhere to lay down, and rest with his best friend, Blake. The two girls were now chatting about the patter of tiny feet. Alex and Brad were still more concerned with what the werewolves might be outside.

"Have you seen or heard anything outside? How has it been for the last hour?" asked Brad.

"At the start of the hour, I could hear movement outside, and it sounded like they were eating out there, but once the snoring started... haven't heard or seen anything though," explained Alex, and then laughs, "I couldn't tell who was snoring loudest over there, Deryck or Carol?"

"Well, it's not me. I haven't been able to sleep!" came a male voice from the other side of the room.

"Hiya Deryck!" Alex and Brad snickered to each other as they watched their girls laugh.

"I'll go over there and keep watch while the girls are chatting... I'll get them to make us a coffee," said Brad as he headed over to the girls.

Alex watched as Brad approached the girls, chattered with them and hugged Amber. Brad then sat down near the window to start his watch. The girls went over to a sideboard, which was set up for hot drinks. They then went back to their men with their coffees. The hour went quick when the band members joined them and relieved them of their watch. The four went over to Alex and Amber first and congratulated them. Glenn and Gary took over their watch, whilst Jon and George walked over to Brad and Lucy.

"Go on, go and get some sleep... we'll take over here," said Jon, as Brad handed him the shotgun.

Brad and Lucy went back to where they had slept before, leaving Jon and George at their post.

Chapter Fifteen

Meanwhile, outside at midnight, two creatures were exhausted after their evening of bloodlust. The moon had been lost through the clouds, and it was raining. The weather on the dales was renowned for changing in an instant. The couple were resting on the other side of a stone wall leading onto one of the lonely fields of the dales. For half an hour they had closed their eyes, but they could not afford to do this for too long, as they would be hunted down at the first opportunity. With only half an hour lost, the pair awoke, wet, cold, naked, and bloody from their gunshot wounds. The moon was still hidden, and the couple had transformed back to their former selves. They needed to flee the area as soon as possible. Climbing over the wall, they crept back to the carpark, where they saw the bodies they had butchered.

"What have we done?" asked the female.

"We cannot think about that now. We need to get out of here as soon as possible… follow me."

The male walked over to Simon's Land Rover, followed by his mate. Luckily, for them, Simon was quite forgetful, and left his vehicle unlocked, and the keys still in the ignition. They climbed inside and started the engine, and then drove out of the carpark.

They headed west, to where they had left their motor home.

"My arm is in agony!"

"See if you can find anything in the back. Anything to help with the bleeding?"

"Wow, this guy comes prepared. There's a lot of first aid stuff here."

"Cool. What we will do is grab our stuff we need, and head to France. Is there a road map anywhere?"

"Yes, he has one of them as well. Bottles of water as well. This guy was in the mountain rescue as well," said the female as she bandaged her wounds.

Not far from the pub, the couple reached their motor home at one.

They finished caring for the female's wounds and got dressed. Gathering what they needed, they got back into the Land Rover.

"Carry on, straight ahead. We can pick up an A road, which will link us to the M6, south. We should be at the channel tunnel by nine o'clock."

"Cool. I think them at the pub will be too scared to leave the pub until the morning. Hopefully, that will give us enough time to escape to France."

"Keep to the speed limit. We cannot draw attention to ourselves. The motorways should hopefully be snow free."

"Ok. Luckily, we have a full tank of gas. How is your arm, and your hand?"

"Still sore, but the pain relief seems to be working. How are you, babe?"

"I'm ok, babe!"

With a well-maintained Land Rover, the couple were able to keep at a steady speed and reached the motorway within an hour of their journey. The motorway was clear of snow, and it was still raining. The moon was still hidden by the clouds, which now needed to be the case until the sunrise. They drove for another four hours until they reached the M25. Time was on their side, but…

"Why have you got Jack's passport?"

"I've been missing for a while. I can't use my passport."

"You can't use this one neither!"

"Look at his eyes and nose. Do you not think he looks like me? Just need to convince them that I have had a shave and a haircut."

"And that you have had your tattoo removed?"

"What?"

"Did you not notice his tattoo on his neck? It is clearly visible in the passport photo."

"Shit, now what are we going to do?"

"I have a marker pen. You'll have to pull over at a service station, and I'll draw the tattoo on your neck. It's a straightforward design."

"Ok, but what about your passport? Were you not missing?"

"I was, only for two days though. I've had a new passport since."

"Oh, ok, sweet!"

The couple continued until they reached the Clacket Lane Service Station and parked for a quick rest. They were now safe from the moon, as the sun was rising. They will keep their human forms now, until the next full moon. She proceeded with drawing the fake tattoo on his neck, which was of a swallow.

"There you go, all done. Maybe I should become a tattoo artist?"

"I don't want any permanent ones, thanks. I'm starving, are you hungry, babe?"

"Yes. Hang on!" she said as she looked in the back and grabbed a plastic box. "Energy bars, fruit. This bloke was always prepared?"

"Great. Let's get back on the road."

"How are we going to pay for the train? We shouldn't use our cards."

"Jack had a bit of cash with him, about a grand. He will not need it anymore. We'll pay cash."

"Ok, fair enough. Let's go!"

The couple left the service station, and re-joined the motorway, and drove for another few miles, before joining the M26, which links the M20 and the channel tunnel. By 9:30, they were on the train to France. About the same time as those at the pub rising from their slumber.

⊶═◄◊►═⊷

Chapter Sixteen

It was about nine in the morning when people started to rise from their slumber, some still looking lost after their weekend of hell. Eddie, Justin, and John, some of the stag party, were still sitting on watch, not that such security measures were needed anymore. The weather had changed for the better, it was no longer snowing or raining, and there was not so much snow on the floor. People were making themselves hot drinks, contemplating what was yet to come. The band had gone outside to see what damage the bus had sustained the night before, from Boris's accident. Nev and Sam Flash, another stag party member, joined the band to help them.

"How's the bus? Can we help?" asked Flash, as he was known to his friends.

"It's fucked. It's not going anywhere!" answered Jon.

"It's only a flat tire," said Flash.

"Yes, but I don't have a spare or the tools to change it."

"Yes, Jon is always prepared for such occasions," laughed Glenn.

"Ha-ha, Glenn. Shut up," replied Jon.

"But there are enough vehicles to get us away from here though, ain't there?" replied Nev.

"Yes, hopefully... we have decided to put the bodies on board the bus... give them a bit more dignity and clear up the scene, so no one comes across such a horrific sight," said Jon.

"Give us a hand?"

"Of course, we will," replied Flash, "who are we having as the driver?"

"Sick joke, not funny... some of these guys are your friends?" said Glenn.

"Sorry, only joking."

"Do you think it is wise to clear the scene, before the police get here?" said Nev.

"Apparently, they are already here," said Gary as he and George carried Detective Coman's body onto the bus.

"Sick! I think, with the snow and the rain, much of the evidence has gone, already. Wouldn't want a family with kids to stumble across such a carnage."

"I suppose not," replied Nev.

They were joined by Deryck, who had been watching them from the pub.

"What are you guys doing? You should have left them where they lay, for the police."

"We thought we would give them a bit of dignity. Plus, you would not want your grandkids to come across such a scene. Nor would any other family," explained George.

"I guess not?"

The group had moved the bodies onto the bus, including Simon's body from the foyer and the three bodies in the courtyard. They also managed to find Boris's mangled body on the road where he fell. The bodies had been placed onto the bunks and the sofa's along the back of the bus. Their bodies had been covered with whatever could be found. However, they had missed one thing, which still sat on the stairs in the foyer.

Deryck then led the group back into the bar to find some breakfast waiting for them, which Tony and Carol had prepared. While everyone had something to eat, the staff sat together, chatting. Half an hour later, Tony stood up and started to address everyone.

"Can I have everyone's attention, please?"

Everyone stopped what they were doing to hear what Tony had to say.

"We are so sorry for what has happened to everyone this weekend... However, we need to leave today. We have enough vehicles, and the weather has turned in our favour. We will start to leave in about an hour." explained Tony, "Deryck and Carol will be heading to Richmond police station to try and explain what has happened here. Everyone needs to leave their name, telephone number and address so that the police can contact you if they need to."

Clare passed around a notebook and pen, so everyone could leave their details.

"It seems like this carnage was caused by the band's roadie and his girlfriend. Whoever or whatever they are, they seem to have fled. Any questions?" said Deryck.

"We are going to Kirby Stephen with my uncle, Brad and Lucy are coming with us... anyone else are welcome to join us," explained Alex, "I want to pick my car up."

"Oh... we need Ruby's gritter to move any snow in the way," replied Tony.

"No, you don't!" snapped Ruby, "my brother is dead because of this place!"

"No, we don't, Tony!" said Deryck, "I'll take my tractor... Jon, you drive your tour bus."

"No, flat tire. I have no spare. Sorry guys."

"Oh. Do you think you can drive Max's lorry outside?"

"Yes, it should be ok," replied Jon.

"Although it rained last night, there is still a lot of snow and slush out there, which I will be able to clear with the tractor," explained Deryck.

"I'll drive my four by four, and we have Simon's Land Rover," said Carol.

"No, we don't!" replied Brad, looking out of the window, "it's gone... it's not outside anymore."

"We are not missing anyone, are we?"

"No, it must have been taken by those werewolves, the roadie and his girl," said Tony.

"We'll take our car... we can fit five. Chloe's brother will come with us," said Gina.

"Right, if everyone is ready, go to your rooms and collect what you need," requested Deryck.

Everyone had finished their breakfasts, and headed up to their rooms to freshen up, and collect their belongings. They were all downstairs, ready, and waiting outside for their mass exodus from the Tan Hill Inn within an hour. The drivers of each vehicle that will be making the journey had started their engines. The others loaded up their designated cars with their luggage.

During this hellish weekend, a strange bond had grown between everyone, and some seem to have forgotten that others tried to cover things up. Many had lost someone they knew and loved during their stay at the Tan Hill Inn.

"You two take care and good luck with your baby. Despite what's happened here, I would love to keep in touch and meet the little one when he or she arrives," said Carol with tears in her eyes as she cuddled Amber and Alex.

Carol then turned to Ruby, "I'm sorry that you and your brother and his colleague got dragged into this mess, Ruby."

"Brad, I'm sorry how this turned out for you. I hope you get answers to what happened to your brother."

"Thank you, Carol. I'm sorry I was horrible to you at the start of this," answered Brad.

"I deserved it!"

"Can I grab a lift from you guys? I live in Kirby Stephen," asked Sam.

"Of course, you can," said Alex.

Sam turned to Carol and hugged her, "thanks for being a great boss, love you and Deryck... going to miss you both, keep in touch?"

"We will... you won't get rid of us as easy as that," replied Carol as she kissed Sam on the cheek. The pair started to cry.

The group climbed into Ruby's lorry, and he drove off, turning left onto the road heading west.

"I'll stay behind so that someone is here for the police. I'll also talk to the people coming to look at your pub, Deryck," said Tony.

"Are you sure, Tony?"

"Yes, you need someone here for them, to explain what's happened... they see this carnage, the buyers will run a mile," explained Tony, "just let the police know that I'm here, and I'm innocent... love you guys, going to miss you."

"We'll keep in touch, Tony. Stay safe," replied Deryck.

The rest of those left in the carpark, did their farewells, and got into their vehicles. Deryck drove his tractor out of the carpark and headed east towards Richmond, leaving the Tan Hill Inn and those who died there behind, with Tony. Everyone else followed Deryck out of the carpark.

The convoy headed off along the road, following Deryck's tractor eastwards until they reached Max's trailer. They had stopped to put Max's body in the back of the trailer. Justin, Nev, and Flash helped Deryck pick up Max's body. Sarah came over and took his hand as they carried him to the back of the trailer. She kissed him one last time as Justin climbed up onto the back of the trailer.

"Ready, take his shoulders, Justin… ok, slide him in gently," said Deryck. "Ok. Thanks, guys."

"Thank you!" said Sarah as she shed a tear.

Deryck took her hand and gave it a loving squeeze, "That's ok, sweetheart. Carol and I loved him, and he was a lovely chap."

The four head back to their vehicles, and Sarah joined Deryck in his tractor.

"He looked peaceful lying there on the trailer… I miss him so much, Deryck."

"You'll get through this, love," replied Deryck, "Let's get going."

The convoy continued with their journey along the Pennine Way. They drove for another ten miles when they came across a Land Rover, heading towards them from the other direction.

"Shit, is that them?" asked Sarah.

"No, Simons Land Rover was a darker colour."

The convoy stopped when they reached the Land Rover, which also pulled over. Deryck got down from his tractor and walked over to them.

"What's he doing?… what if that's them?" said Justin, who had joined Carol in her car, along with Lisa and Clare, after they had finished putting Max on the trailer.

"That's not Simon's Land Rover," said Clare.

"Who is it then?" asked Lisa.

"Might be the people who are buying our pub?"

Deryck approached the driver's door and tapped on the window. There were three people in the vehicle, two men in the front and a woman sitting in the back. The driver opened his window and greeted Deryck.

"Hiya."

"Hiya guys, where are you heading to?" asked Deryck

"We're heading to the Tan Hill Inn," said the driver.

"Ahhh, ok... are you, Andrew and Mike... you're looking at buying the pub?"

"Yes, we are... why?"

"I'm Deryck, the landlord... that there driving that car, is Carol, my wife... there has been a serious incident at the pub this weekend," explained Deryck. "The phone lines are down. We have been stuck there since Friday. We're now heading to Richmond police station to explain what has happened."

"What the fuck... is the pub still there... is it still for sale?" asked Mike, who sat in the passenger seat.

"Yes, we want a quick sale because of what we have been through, we are dropping the price by one hundred grand, and you have the first refusal. There's a bit of work that needs doing, but not that much, and we just want to retire," said Deryck.

"Wow. Well, we are definitely interested," said Andrew.

"Here are my keys. You are more than welcome to go to the pub. Our chef, Tony, is still there," replied Deryck, "but the police will be there soon, once we let them know... the danger has gone now... who's this in the back?"

"This is Maria. She is our duty manager."

"Hiya Maria... some staff hope to keep their jobs. Is that something you would be looking at doing," asked Deryck, "we didn't have any management in place?"

"That's something we would be interested in," said Maria.

"Anyway, I'm going... we've had the shit kicked out of us this weekend," said Deryck, trying not to give too much away.

"What happened?" asked Mike.

"Tony will explain... I will be in touch. I'm looking forward to doing business with you," said Deryck as he walked back to his tractor.

The convoy headed off again on their journey to Richmond, leaving the Land Rover sitting there on its own.

The three sat there for a while to discuss their options.

"What the fuck!" said Andrew.

"Shall we still take a look?" asked Maria

"Not sure if we should!" replied Andrew.

"Well, we've got to turn around anyway, and we're close... we might as well turn around there... just have a look to see what has happened. It won't hurt," said Mike.

"Come on, let's go," replied Andrew.

He started the engine, and they headed off towards the Tan Hill Inn. They drove for another ten minutes when they came across the trailer, and what Deryck told them of the weekend's events started to unravel.

"What's that lorry doing there?... looks like it's been broken into," uttered Maria.

"We'll take a look, Maria... you stay in the car... please?" asked Mike.

Andrew and Mike got out of their vehicle and went to the back of the trailer and looked inside.

"What's that? It looks like a pair of feet!" said Andrew. He then turned his attention to Max's body, not knowing who or what the situation was. "Hey, you ok in there, mate... you need a hand?"

"Here, give me a foot up, Andrew," said Mike, "I'll see if he's ok."

"Everything ok?" asked Maria as she joined the pair.

"Not sure, there's a bloke in there... Mike is seeing if we can help."

On inspection, Mike fell backwards, shocked by what he found. He was not expecting such a scene.

"What is it?"

"He's frozen solid, but that's not what killed him... looks as if some sort of large dog has attacked him," replied Mike, "let's get out of here."

The three went back to their vehicle and returned to their journey to the pub.

They stayed silent until they got to the carpark, where they found Tony standing outside. He waved to them, and Andrew parked beside him and opened his window.

"Hiya guys, can I help you? Are you the police? I'm surprised you got here that quick."

"No, we're not. I'm Andrew, this is Mike and that is Maria. We are here about the pub. Can you show us around?"

The three got out of their vehicle, and properly introduced themselves to Tony.

"Wow, a coach. Is it yours?" asked Andrew.

"I wouldn't go in there if... too late. It's not our coach, it belongs to the band who were playing here, this weekend."

Andrew climbed into the coach, and a few seconds later he rushed out. He crouched at the side of the coach, holding on as he vomited onto the ground.

"What's the matter, Andrew?" asked Maria.

"Give me a second," said Andrew as he vomited again. He then cleaned his mouth with his handkerchief.

"Are you ok, what is it?"

"Let's have a look," said Mike.

"Wait, don't go in there. It's full of dead bodies," warned Andrew, "they have been mutilated. Some of them have had their heads cut off."

Inquisitive, Mike climbed onto the first step, to have a look. He was not as quick as Andrew to get off the bus. He vomited straight away, onto the driver's seat.

"I told you guys, not to go on there," said Tony, "are you sure you want to have a look around the pub?"

"Yes, let's have a look around. I need a glass of water, please," said mike as he wiped his mouth with his sleeve.

"Ok, we'll use the porch, rather than the main entrance."

The porch was halfway along the pub, left of the main entrance.

"No thanks, we would like to go through the main entrance."

"Ok, if you insist. Follow me. Mind the floor."

Tony opened the front door, which was splatted in blood, for the three to enter the pub. He had already moved the table barricade, ready for the police. They walked into the foyer and stopped in their tracks because of the sight of Simon's blood on the stone floor. Maria was just able to stop herself stepping in the blood. They all walked around the blood and walked over to the reception. Stopping to look at the office door on the floor, covered in the blood of the female werewolf. They turned and headed up the stairs and stopped at the window which had Paul's blood splatted on the panes of glass. Maria continued up the stairs, and then screamed.

"Are you ok, Maria?"

"There's a head on that step!" she cried as she ran down the stairs.

Tony looked, the band had forgot to find Paul's head, and it still sat where it had landed.

"It's Paul, one of the victims. Sorry about that Maria."

"I think we are going to be making some changes around here if we buy. That window will be bricked up straight away, and the main entrance," said Andrew.

Something outside distracted them as they looked out of the window.

"What's that noise?" Mike said, "it's a helicopter, a police helicopter. It's landing."

"I think we need to go?" replied Andrew.

The four of them headed back outside, and walked towards Mike's Land Rover, just as the helicopter landed on the field opposite the pub. Four men climbed out of the helicopter and headed across the road to the carpark. Two of the men were in uniform, and the other two were in plain clothes. They walked over to the group standing in the carpark. One of the plain clothed officers pointed towards the coach and said something to the others. The other plain clothed officer, and one of the uniformed officers headed in that direction. They disappeared onto the coach.

"Right, which one of you gentlemen, is Tony."

"I am."

"Who are you, guys?" the officer asked the other three.

"I'm Mike, this is Andrew and Maria. We have only just arrived, sir."

"Do you know anything about what has gone one around here?"

"No, sir. Can we go?" asked Andrew.

"Sit in your vehicle and wait until we have finished with you."

Andrew, Mike, and Maria got back into their car as the officer continued to question Tony. Tony was in shock, when the officer read him his rights, and arrested him.

In the distance, the sound of sirens could be heard as a convoy of police vehicles moved along the road, towards the pub. As the convoy turned into the carpark, the last two police cars continued along the road, west towards Kirby Stephen.

⊷⊶⊲◊⊳⊷⊶

Chapter Seventeen

Meanwhile, two hours earlier on the road in the opposite direction of everyone else, a lorry ploughed through what was left of the snow and slush. Ruby headed west, to Kirby Stephen, with his nephew, Alex, and his pregnant wife, Amber. Brad, Lucy, and Sam were sitting in the back, keeping Blake company. Now they had left the Tan Hill Inn; there was a sense of relief.

"What happens now?" asked Alex.

"I guess we wait and hear from the police," answered Ruby.

"Do you know any of Uncle Paul's colleagues we can get in touch with, Uncle Ruby?"

"I know a couple, but I don't have any numbers for them... do you have any signal?" replied Ruby.

"No... anyone else?"

"No, nothing," answered Brad, "I guess, like what Uncle Ruby said, we wait to hear from the police... it's just a relief to get away from that place."

"Those poor souls who we left behind!" said Lucy.

"James and Simon!" muttered Sam as she started to cry.

Lucy put her arm around Sam to comfort her, and Blake snuggled his head into Sam's lap.

"Ah, what a lovely dog," said Sam as she kissed Blake.

They drove for another five minutes when they spotted something ahead of them, which looked like a van.

"Wait, is that the roadie's mobile home up there, bud?" expressed Brad.

"It looks like it," answered Alex.

"What is it doing parked there? Can you see anyone?"

"No, Uncle Ruby, I can't see anyone. Looks peaceful, and all locked up," said Brad.

"Why do you keep calling him Uncle Ruby, Brad?"

"I thought that was his name, bro?"

"It is, but he's my uncle."

"Hey, buddy, he's everyone's uncle after this weekend. Your uncle is amazing."

"Oh, ok, I can live with that, Brad."

"So, can I, Brad," replied Ruby, "we need to stop, and take a look. Hopefully, we can apprehend these bastards before they can change again."

"Apprehend them, we need to kill them. So, they can't do more killing, bud," said Brad.

"And how would we explain that to the police?" replied Alex, "we'll end up in prison ourselves."

Ruby pulled up alongside the van and turned off the engine. Alex got out first, followed by Brad. Ruby loaded his shotgun, got out and joined the other two.

"Girls, stay in the lorry!" insisted Ruby.

The three men looked around the van and then went to the front to see through the windscreen.

"Looks as though they just parked up here, rather than skidding off the road?" revealed Brad.

"I can't see anything through the windscreen... we need to look inside," answered Alex, "If they took the Land Rover, why did they leave this here?"

The three of them headed for the side door and found it locked. Ruby went back to the driver's door and tried the handle, only to find that that was also locked. He took off his jacket and wrapped it around his right hand. Alex and Brad looked at each other, puzzled. Placing his shotgun on the floor, he picked up a large stone, smashed the driver's window, and opened the door. Ruby picked up his shotgun, and quickly opened the door. He climbed into the vehicle and moved to the back. Ruby then hesitated once he saw the scene in the back. He then opened the side door for his nephew and Brad.

"There's a dead body in here... blood everywhere... I'm no expert, but he looks as though he's been sitting here for a while... his wrists have been cut. Blood is no longer flowing from his wounds, and some as dried out."

Alex and Brad entered the van to see the dead body sitting on the sofa along the back of the vehicle. His blood covered the sofa and floor around him. There was also splattering's of blood on the walls.

"What the fuck... it's that roadie, Jack. He's slashed his own wrists," declared Brad.

"Look at his stomach. He's cut himself open like ritual suicide. The band said Jack was into the Samurai culture," said Alex, "Brad, this is Seppuku. What I was telling you about yesterday."

"Fuck, what a gruesome way to die. How did he do that to himself after slitting his wrists?"

"That would explain the Samurai sword on that wall, over there," answered Ruby.

"And there's a smaller one on the floor, here... covered in blood," replied Brad.

"That's the Wakizashi. Hang on... if Jack has been here all that long, who was the second werewolf last night?" asked Alex, "there were definitely two of them last night."

Brad, on his search, had found a familiar looking bag, which made nervous.

"I think I know!" disclosed Brad as he picked up the backpack, "this looks like my brothers."

Brad opened the bag and started to empty the contents onto the sofa, away from Jack's body.

"Shit, this is Karl's stuff... fuck, is he the other werewolf?" Brad was stunned as he sat down and started to cry, "Is this all my fault? I shouldn't have let him go ahead of me."

"Shit, are you sure it's Karl's stuff?" Lucy said from the door as she joined them, "you weren't to know, babe."

"Yes, it's his... I thought I saw him in this van when they drove away Saturday morning," uttered Brad, "he's left my map in his bag... he's left me a message... 'I'll see you soon brother... sorry'," read Brad, "what does that mean?"

"What do you think he is up to?" asked Alex.

"He's leaving the country... I think he's carrying on with our journey around Europe, using these maps. I wonder if he has left me any clues to where he is going."

"Hang on, this other sword... it's also covered in blood," said Ruby as he removed the sword from its case.

"What the fuck was this used for, then?" Alex asked as he took the sword from his uncle to examine its quality and ethnicity. Ruby then walked to the front of the vehicle and had a search around.

"Bloody hell, this sword is old. It could be worth a lot of money?" said Alex.

"It's also evidence. It would be best if you put it back, Alex. We need to get out of here before anyone else turns up," replied Lucy.

Alex put the sword back on the wall and got his phone out to check the time. He then put his phone down.

"Come on, everyone. Lucy is right. We don't want to be here when the police get here."

Whilst searching at the front of the van, Ruby found something that might give up some vital clues to the group.

"Hey, guys. I found a phone. It was left here on charge."

"Wow, who's could that be?" said Alex.

The phone suddenly rings as a familiar ringtone fills the van. The phone played the American national anthem, and Ruby answered it.

"Hello?"

"It's my brother's phone," said Brad as he cancelled the call. "Give it to me, Uncle Ruby?"

Ruby handed the phone to Brad, and Brad entered Karl's password to unlock the phone.

"Yes, this is definitely Karl's cell phone. There's a couple of unread messages here."

"Oh, anything to do with what has happened this weekend?" said Lucy.

"No. Seems as though Karl met these two guys on his journey here. Actually, there may be a link with the second guy."

"How do you mean?" asked Alex.

"The first guy, called Steve, served Karl in a bar at Kings Cross station. He talks about meeting Karl and I in France, near a place where we were planning on visiting," explained

Brad. "The second guy, Karl met on the train. He's asking Karl if he has any news on his missing sister... Tanya."

"Shit, that's the woman who was with him, sitting there," said Lucy as she pointed at Jack.

"Come on. I think we better get out of here, before the police turn up," said Ruby.

The group climbed back into Ruby's lorry and then continued their journey to Kirby Stephen. Another ten minutes passed when they reached Alex's car.

"There she is. She looks ok sitting there, hopefully she'll start?"

"Look, I'll park in front of your car, and I'll tow her back onto the road."

"Thanks, Uncle."

Ruby towed the vehicle from where it had settled on the side of the road. Luckily, there was not a lot of damage, just a few scratches and dents. Alex turned the key, and the engine started for the first time.

"Oh, thank fuck for that," said Alex, "shit, I've left my phone back at the van. You guys head off, and I'll catch you up. Amber, you stay with them. It won't take me long. I'll see you in a bit."

Before anyone else could say anything, Alex turned around and drove back to the mobile home.

Once Alex was back at the mobile home, he quickly climbed back into the van and picked up his phone. However, it was not the phone he wanted. That was a ploy. He had really gone back to collect the Samurai swords. He picked up a sharp carving knife, smeared the swords' blood onto it, and then smeared Jack's blood onto it. He then placed the carving knife at Jack's feet. Alex found a cloth and some cleaning products and cleaned the blood off the blades and left the van with them. When Alex placed his find in his boot, he noticed a label with a name and a mobile number on one of the cases. The label said '*Tanya, look after my swords, love Peter xx*'

"I wonder who Peter is? Must be the same chap who had messaged Brad's brother," Alex said to himself as he covered the swords with a blanket. Alex had also placed a binbag into his boot, which contained the cloth he had used to clean the blades. He got back in his car and drove to catch up with the others.

The End…. or is it?

Lightning Source UK Ltd.
Milton Keynes UK
UKHW021323190123
415612UK00008B/117